ALSO BY ADAM ROSS

Mr. Peanut

Ladies and Gentlemen

Ladies and Gentlemen

ADAM ROSS

Alfred A. Knopf · New York · 2011

THIS IS A BORZOI BOOK
PUBLISHED BY ALFRED A. KNOPF

Knopf, Borzoi Books, and the colophon are
registered trademarks of Random House, Inc.

Library of Congress Cataloging-in-Publication Data
Ross, Adam, 1967–
Ladies and gentlemen / by Adam Ross.—1st ed.
p.   cm.
ISBN 978-0-307-27071-9
1. Title.
PS3618.O84515L33 2011
813'.6—dc22   2011006960

Jacket photograph © Tom Schierlitz / Getty Images
Jacket design by Gabrielle Brooks

Manufactured in the United States of America
First Edition

To Jon Glover and Sara Hill Glover

Cruelty, like every other vice, requires no motive outside of itself; it only requires opportunity.

—*George Eliot*

CONTENTS

Futures 3

The Rest of It 65

The Suicide Room 101

In the Basement 129

When in Rome 149

Middleman 187

Ladies and Gentlemen 227

Ladies and Gentlemen

Futures

Before the interview—in one of his two appropriate suits, this one a blue pinstripe—David Applelow, aged forty-three, passed the time forecasting: predicting first what his interviewer might look like, hoping for a beautiful woman, not merely attractive but uncommonly gorgeous, who would not only be so kind as to give him a job (that is, save his life) but also to offer herself as an immediate bonus, on the desk or the rug (if there was one) or the chair if it had no arms, her offer an act of the greatest generosity, because this kind of thing, however common to a man's fantasy, never happened, particularly not to Applelow, and if it were to, he would be surprised for the first time in years.

And then he suddenly became self-critical. It was typical, cripplingly typical, Applelow thought, for his mind to wander just before an interview, like being unserious when just the opposite was called for. And so, after a stern, internal upbraiding, a pinch to the crease in his pants, and the discovery and timely plucking of black string sticking out from the heel of his loafer, he considered the questions he might be asked when he finally *did* step through that door. He hoped to forge an immediate connection with the woman; as on a good first date, they would get beyond the scripted questions and move gingerly toward something more personal, such as his opinions on how things really worked or insights gleaned from his stints as a professional. And then they'd hedge toward the future. She'd talk about the job as if it were his already, about benefits, profit sharing, and salary—a number exceeding even his most optimistic expectations—and thus the accident that had brought him to this office would reveal itself to have been fated.

His mind wandered again, and he felt disembodied, adrift. Ceiling high, he watched himself sitting there. *Walk,* he thought. A soda might give him the boost he needed, but he foresaw a devastating, midinterview belch. He was unbearably hungry. To take his mind off his appetites, he picked up the nearest magazine.

When Applelow had arrived earlier, two men were waiting in the reception area. One was younger, in his midtwenties, underdressed in jeans and a golf shirt, with a résumé in his lap that appeared to be handwritten. He was a bundle of tics, pulling at his nose and snorting repeatedly, as if gathering up enough mucus to hawk it out. The second candidate, an enormous black man in a cheap gray suit, made a production of working on his laptop to pass the time—no easy trick, as his digits were so thick he had to type single-fingered—and then made several calls on his cell phone that Applelow was sure were fake. At one point, he turned to the receptionist, whose nameplate read *Madeline,* and said:

"Excuse me. A matter of protocol. I have two résumés, one with a more technical focus on my specialty and the other leaning toward more personal qualifications. Is there a particular aspect you'd prefer we stress?"

Which told Applelow that he had no competition in the room. Madeline, slowly swiveling around in her chair, replied, "Whichever you'd rather we see." With a flourish, the man opened his briefcase and reviewed both résumés, then decided on one with a determined nod of the head. The younger man two chairs down from Applelow pumped his heel up and down so fiercely it shook the seat between them. Then he suddenly got up and left.

Applelow raised an eyebrow at Madeline.

"It's not the first time," she said.

Gray Suit was called into the office. A few minutes later he too was headed out.

It was a chance, Applelow thought, to get some information, because the ad for this job had been mysterious. A few days ago, while searching the classifieds, he'd spilled coffee on the newspaper, the liquid forking out and rejoining to cast one small section of the newsprint into dry relief. He was about to clean up his mess when the headline caught his eye.

THE FUTURE IS NOW

Are you perceptive, analytical, a troubleshooter? Have excellent interpersonal skills you were never sure how to parlay into $$$? Auratec is a fast-growing, highly selective West Coast company seeking applicants with ability in the abstract to help us start offices in the New York area. Will train qualified candidates. SALARY AND BENEFITS. 401(K). Growth potential unlimited. Fax résumé attention Laura Samuel. 556-1583.

"Have you seen a lot of people for the job already?" he asked Madeline.

She turned from her computer to give him her full attention. On the wall behind her a sign said *Auratec,* with an Egyptian ankh in place of the *t.* "Ms. Samuel has been seeing people constantly."

Applelow waited, smiling.

"We're always growing," she continued.

"It's a small office."

"Our new one's being renovated at the Time Warner building."

"Ah," Applelow said.

The phone burbled quietly, but she didn't answer it.

"So is this a sales position?"

Madeline winced sweetly. "I'm afraid I can't give out that information."

Of course not, Applelow thought.

Earlier that afternoon, he'd withdrawn twenty-four hundred dollars from his bank account—every cent he had—in hundred-dollar bills. In his current financial straits, he felt the need to have the cash on hand, and there was something liberating about keeping all your assets on your person. He imagined it must be how a camel feels about its hump. Afterward, he walked down Fifth Avenue to the interview feeling strangely confident, among the lunch crowds and tourists. He played catch-her-eye with beautiful women and noted his reflection in shop windows, appearing to anyone concerned like someone who had a place in the world. This heady feeling carried him to the Rockefeller rink, where he stopped to watch the children skate, watched their parents watching them, and stared at the lovers holding hands. But then his mood darkened and he leaned against the railing, crushed with despair.

It was not uncommon for Applelow to be poor. He'd made real money during only a few brief stretches. His working life had been a hodgepodge of "professions"—a few years as a corporate speechwriter, as an assistant to a literary editor, as a set builder for a film-production company. Not every job he'd had was a dead end, but none had ever gelled into anything that could be called a career. He'd spent the last six years managing a small off-Broadway theater company called The Peanut Gallery, founded and funded by an actor named Jason Heywood Green, whose career in independent films, despite sterling reviews, had lately taken a dive. "I'm playing the heavy in the *Mission Impossible* sequel just to make my mortgage payments," he'd told Applelow. "My accountant says I've got to trim some fat." So, in the blink of an eye, the place where Applelow thought he'd spend the next decade of his professional life was shut down, and after his unemployment benefits ran out he burned through what little savings he had in a matter of months. The company had done three productions every year, and he'd handled everything from marketing and advertising to set building and accounting. There was almost nothing with which he hadn't had some sort of experience, but his applications went unanswered and the terrible economy didn't help. It was a world, he was realizing, divided between the specialized and the unspecialized, the job titles all the more convoluted the less specialized they were. Applelow was starting to fear that this recent turn of events was in fact the beginning of a slide into unrecoverable failure. You should have seen this coming, he thought.

Madeline's intercom chimed. "Yes, Ms. Samuel?"

"If I don't eat soon," the voice said, "I'm going to kill some-body."

Madeline looked at Applelow and shrugged her shoulders apol-ogetically. She turned off the intercom, and picked up the handset. "Yes," she said, lowering her voice. "No, he doesn't."

"I can wait," Applelow whispered.

But the door was already opening.

"It's an eclectic résumé," Ms. Samuel said.

"That's how I like to think of it," Applelow answered.

To call Ms. Samuel gorgeous would have been a titanic under-statement. She was one of the most beautiful women he had ever seen: young, blonde, twenty-eight at most, and positively tiny—maybe five foot two in heels—with owlish gray eyes. Everything in her office radiated a spare, modern seriousness, yet her demeanor was disarmingly warm. She listened to Applelow's initial answers with a polished professionalism, but when their banter turned light, she punctuated it with musical little tee-hees.

"Feature film releasing?" she asked.

"B-picture distribution," Applelow said. "This was to theaters in the Times Square area. Horrible stuff. *Apache Ninja. Jailhouse Jane.* This was a long time ago. Back in the late eighties."

"It says here you were VP of the whole division."

"Well, there was just the boss and me. We were the whole com-pany. Consequently, I was VP of everything. VP of phone, VP of faxes. VP of copies."

Ms. Samuel tee-heed. Snorted loudly.

He loved her.

"Canvassing coordinator," she said. "Tell me about that."

"It was a fund-raising campaign for toxic-cleanup legislation on Long Island. You'll see I grossed more in donations that year than anyone else in my division. It was pure sales—one of the great think-on-your-feet jobs. Take information about an issue, then develop your own rap out of it. Leave a stranger's door with money."

Applelow was on the ball. He didn't sell his good qualities too hard. Without sounding like a liability, he addressed weaknesses that could be transformed into strengths. When they talked about his tenure at the theater company he was so on point he would have hired himself. It was a *waltz,* Applelow thought, with Ms. Samuel leading, but it was also like dancing in a pitch-dark room. What was the job?

"Okay," she said. "Let's take this in another direction." Ms. Samuel came around to the front of her desk and leaned against it. "Do you put much stock in astrology?"

"The science?"

Ms. Samuel started pacing. "Zodiac, stars, the whole thing. Do you believe it has any merit at all?"

This question gave him serious pause. Could she be a horoscope nut or a chart maker? What if astrology was her personal religion?

"I'm an Aquarius," he answered safely.

"Terrific. I'm a Leo. But do you *buy* it?"

If he didn't, was he out of the running? If he did, was he a loon? "Sometimes," he said.

"Meaning what?"

"Meaning," he continued, "that if I'm on line at the supermarket, I'll give my horoscope a glance."

"A*ha*," she said, and pointed at him.

"But it's not a daily thing," he assured her.

"But when you *do* look at it," she said, "and the forecast is negative, what's your reaction?"

"Honestly?" She didn't look offended by this. "I discount it," he answered truthfully.

"Exactly. What about a *good* forecast?"

"Then things are looking up!" he said, and smiled.

When Ms. Samuel didn't smile back, he became serious again. *Listening.*

"What about tarot?" she said, pacing. "Ever consult the cards?"

"No."

"The prophecies of Nostradamus?"

"Haven't read him."

"Believe in past lives? Reincarnation? What about karma?"

Already this was the strangest interview of his whole life. "No to all three."

"What about ESP?"

I want to fuck you cross-eyed.

Ms. Samuel waited impassively.

"Not anymore," he said.

"All right. Let's try this one." She pressed her index finger to her mouth and tapped it.

It was like the moment in a play, Applelow thought, right before the offstage gunshot.

"Have you felt," she said, "for a long time, perhaps for as long as you can remember, that something good was coming your way? You couldn't say what it might be, but you've always believed it."

Applelow's heart was racing.

"Have you believed that this life—right here, right now—wasn't the one you thought you'd be living?" She leaned toward him. "That there was something bigger for you. You were sure of it. You *are* sure of it. Do you know what I'm talking about, David? Do you know what I *mean?*"

He felt himself pressing into the chair back. Looking at her was like looking into brilliant light. "Yes," he said.

"*Good,*" she said. "Good, David. Now we're getting somewhere."

Applelow called the employment agency he was working with and canceled the interviews they'd scheduled for the rest of the afternoon. The man who'd been sending him out—Tom Pard—laid into him. He told Applelow he *knew* he'd do this and should've trusted his gut when they met, that he could tell from the get-go he wouldn't make it through a single day of hitting the street.

Applelow hung up on him and, thinking of the million things he could've said to Pard in response, adjusted his tie in a store window's reflection, licked his finger to smooth his light eyebrows, and pushed up his eyeglasses. He narrowed his fox eyes, trying to remember what he looked like before he'd lost most of his hair. No, he thought, no more interviews today. No more questions, no more performing. Enough was simply enough.

On the bus, he began criticizing himself again. Pard was right.

He was soft, lazy, unfocused. So what if he'd had a good interview, that he had a *feeling* about this job—whatever it was. It was oh so typical of him not to explore all the possibilities, to instead latch on to the good thing that came his way (and it hadn't come just yet, he reminded himself). He could apologize, admit that he was wrong, then go on an interview or two after he ate. He jumped up from his seat and pressed the bell. But calling the man back was impossible, and the driver, shooting him a look in the mirror, flashed past his stop. When Applelow turned to sit down again, he saw that an elderly woman had already taken his seat.

Monday.

But he was sure that his interview with Ms. Samuel had gone well. "David," she'd said, "it's been a unique pleasure talking with you. Positively unique." She walked him briskly to the door. Left no choice, he finally asked what the job was exactly.

Ms. Samuel grimaced. "We're not at that point yet," she said.

"Can't you tell me anything?"

"We work in media. Sociological research. Also entertainment."

"I've spent years in entertainment," he said, kicking himself immediately. Ms. Samuel ushered him forward and opened the door. The waiting room was now entirely full of young, handsome people wearing appropriate suits.

"You'll hear from me," Ms. Samuel said. "Probably by Wednesday."

Her hand, when he shook it, was ice-cold.

Applelow's apartment was on 44th Street between Ninth and Tenth, a large one-bedroom on the second floor of a four-story walk-up—rent-controlled, thank God—that he'd lived in for seven years. He knew all of his neighbors, and approaching the building, he saw Mrs. Gunther, a thick little turtle of a woman, standing on the stoop in her housecoat, holding two full trash bags. Muttering, she dragged them down the steps. Applelow didn't want to talk to her, but he was sure she'd seen him. He said hello as he hurried past, flipping through his keys at the front door. "Vhat?" she said, and kicked the bags against the trash cans. Then she began to labor up the steps behind him. For years he'd brought her trash down for her—she lived alone on the fourth floor and had an arthritic hip—but since things had taken a bad turn this weekly generosity had been neglected.

"Goot you hev your key," she said. "I left mine in apartmint."

Applelow held the door open for her, and when she paused halfway up the first flight and rubbed her hip he grudgingly walked her to the top floor. They didn't speak, nor did she thank him when they arrived at her door. And after starting back down, he promised himself, Never again.

As he turned down the third-floor landing, he saw Marnie Kastopolis, his next-door neighbor, waiting for him below.

"I heard you come in," she said as he descended. She blinked once and smiled broadly, revealing her thick, white teeth. Marnie was tall, nearly six feet, and painfully awkward. She was wide-hipped and narrow-chested, a long-legged redhead whose odd proportions reminded Applelow of a Giacometti. She needed something from him now, but her efforts at sultriness were a caricature even more painful because she was wholly unaware of their effect. Or perhaps it was because he was still uncomfortable around her. Several weeks ago, after sharing two bottles of wine in her apartment, Applelow had tried to kiss her. While she was laughing at something he'd said, he'd lunged forward and hit her teeth when he put his lips to hers. He was sure she'd wanted him to, but the moment he did it she put her hands on his shoulders and, with their lips still pressed together, told him no. "Not that I'm not flattered," she said, pushing him back. He apologized profusely and stood up, so furious he could barely see, and left soon after. They hadn't spoken about the incident since.

"I need a favor," Marnie said.

Applelow waited.

"Zach's coming down from school tonight." This was Marnie's youngest son. "And I have to go to work." A concierge at one of the luxury hotels near Times Square, she often worked nights. "Can you let him in?" She held up her key. "Just, please, be sure to take it back afterward."

"Just open the door and let him in?"

"Yes."

"You don't trust him with the key?"

Marnie crossed her arms and looked down at the floor. "If he's in, I want to *know* he's in. If he's going out, he has to let me *know*."

If the fact that she didn't trust her son was going to be an evening-long obligation, *he* wanted to know *that*. "Has it been that bad?" he said.

"No," she answered, and looked up. "He's getting it together, David." She said this automatically, her tone aping conviction, and she must have noticed the doubt on his face. "I really mean it this time."

"Terrific."

"He's joining the air force," Marnie offered. "He's doing basic training in California at the end of the semester. He says he wants to fly jets."

Who doesn't? Applelow thought. "You must be relieved."

"Words," she said, looking up, "do not describe."

"So trust him," he said, though he regretted it immediately. He had no plans tonight. Helping her out wouldn't cost him a thing.

Marnie looked at her shoe for a moment, checking the heel, the leather's shine. "I've left some dinner in the refrigerator for the both of you," she said. "There's even some cake."

"Lovely."

"I'll put a note on the front door for him to buzz you. His bus gets in at seven."

"I'll be here."

"Thank you," she mouthed, and placed the key in his outstretched palm.

The truth was that Applelow had always been curious about Marnie's second child, whom he'd never met. He *had* met the oldest son, Aaron. "My little genius," she called him. He was both: little and a genius. Exactly like her husband, she'd explained, who was a diminutive Greek mathematics prodigy. Aaron had inherited his father's gift for cogitation and was on a full scholarship in philosophy at a university upstate, "admitted to the doctoral program at the age of seventeen," Marnie liked to brag. (The brilliant husband had deserted the family long ago.) Applelow had met the boy at Marnie's door last year; he was oddly attracted to her, so he'd feigned interest in the introduction. The boy was the spitting image of his mother, though his head, which was enormous, only came up to her breasts. She turned Aaron toward him, resting her hands on his shoulders, and said, "Here he is!" After the three of them stood there uncomfortably for a moment, Applelow mentioned that he'd heard Aaron was quite the scholar. He was secretly hoping for a performance of some kind, for a monologue on systematic reasoning to come streaming from Aaron's mouth—but the boy just frowned and mumbled hello. Deformed, Applelow thought, frozen boy-sized by so much mama-love.

But it was Zach who kept Marnie up at night. Though she slaved away keeping both boys in private schools, Zach had been kicked out of one for cheating, another for shoplifting, and was then shipped off to an out-of-state institution for troubled youths. He was almost expelled for marijuana possession but finally managed to graduate and got into one of the SUNY schools, where he was currently a sophomore on probation for poor grades and considering dropping out. All this had caused Marnie endless worry. "He's going to waste everything," she'd told Applelow during their wine-drinking session.

But all that was in the past, apparently. Zach was joining the air force, aiming high, getting it together. Not enough to be trusted with the key to his mother's apartment, but there was no telling how far he might go.

At home, Applelow checked his messages—there were none—and put his cash in a book on one of his shelves. From his window he watched Marnie walk up the street and turn the corner, then went across the hall and let himself into her apartment. She'd made meatloaf and a salad, but his sweet tooth was acting up so he tore off a huge piece of coffee cake, eating it in front of the open refrigerator and drinking milk out of the carton, taking such enormous bites he had to inhale loudly through his nose. Full, he went back to his apartment and lay down in front of the television. On the news, images from Abu Ghraib: a naked Iraqi with his back to a cell, his genitals pinched between his legs and his hands cupped behind his neck while dogs strained toward him on their leashes. Another prisoner stood on a box, electrodes attached to his fingers and penis, looking like a sort of Ku Klux Klansman in his eyeless, pointy hood. A faceless orgy of captives with a female MP lying atop them like a sister on her brothers' pileup, the blue-gloved guard behind them giving a thumbs-up with a look of sick glee.

Who makes such people? Applelow wondered.

He woke to the sound of the buzzer.

Zach was tall like his mother but better-proportioned, long and lean. He had dark cropped hair and thick black eyebrows. Handsome, Applelow thought. He wore a down jacket over a hooded sweatshirt, jeans, and high-tops, and had a small bag thrown over his shoulder. He apologized for disturbing him, and when Applelow looked in the mirror above his coat rack he saw his throw-pillow's weave imprinted on his cheek.

"No, no," he told the boy. "I needed to wake up." He looked on the counter for Marnie's key, checked under his mail, and then found it in his pants pocket, holding it up as if it were solid gold. After they crossed the hall, Applelow unlocked the door and held it open. The boy waited.

"The key," Zach finally said.

"I'm sorry?" Applelow asked, suddenly furious with Marnie for putting him in this position. She hadn't told the boy that he was under house arrest.

"Ohhhh," Zach said, nodding. He tossed his bag on the floor. "Don't sweat it." He collapsed on the couch and folded his hands over his stomach. He grinned. "I'm surprised she didn't ask you to lock me in from the outside."

Applelow laughed. "I'm guessing she locked the liquor cabinet too."

"Mom doesn't have any booze. She's a true Jew that way." Cackling to himself, he seemed in good spirits. "I could go for a beer, though."

"I'm out," Applelow said, though he'd immediately warmed to the boy.

"I've got some cash."

"No, I'll pay," he said, then went to his apartment and took the book down. When he turned around, Zach was standing in the doorway, looking at his far wall, which was covered with framed posters of productions The Peanut Gallery had done over the years.

"*Cool* place," he said.

"Thank you." Applelow looked at the posters. Better days. "Here." He handed Zach a hundred-dollar bill. "Since I'm warden."

"I'm not *that* thirsty."

"Break it for me."

"What do you like?"

"What do you drink?"

"Whatever."

"Me too," Applelow said.

A few minutes later, the kid came back with a six-pack of Budweiser and handed him the same crisp bill.

"What's this?" he asked.

"I said I had money." Zach went back to the wall and read the posters. "Are you an actor?"

"No, I managed that theater company."

"What do you do now?"

"Now," Applelow said, "I look for work." Zach turned to him. "We closed down."

"Sorry."

"It was a good run."

Sipping seriously, Zach nodded. "I admire that."

"What?"

"That attitude: Enjoy it while it lasts."

"I'd have preferred it lasted a little longer."

"Yeah, well, it's rare, though. That it lasts, I mean. And what you did."

Applelow had never thought of anything he'd done as being particularly rare.

"I'm serious," Zach said. "You're the first manager of a theater company I've ever met. That's unique. The job, I mean. I want to do unique things."

Unique things, Applelow thought, had put him over a void. He could begin a long, cynical monologue now, but instead finished his beer. "Like what?" he said.

"I don't know. I wouldn't mind joining Special Forces. I'm

strong. I have a high pain threshold. I'm thinking everyone hates America so much now that I'll always be busy blowing shit up. Plus I'd get to travel. Go to Europe or the Middle East or something. See some action."

For a moment, Applelow considered his failure to ever leave the country. Possibly he never would. "Not a bad idea," he said.

"I think, though," Zach continued, "I might go work in a cannery in Alaska. Or fish there. This guy I know at school's on a king-crab boat every winter break and makes, like, fifty thousand dollars. Can you believe that? Fifty-fucking-grand."

"That must be dangerous work."

"Extremely."

"Plus Alaska's cold," Applelow pointed out.

"Not for long, with all this global-warming shit."

"True enough."

" 'Cause nothing lasts," Zach said.

"Also true."

"Here's to nothing lasting."

They clinked cans.

"Damn," Zach said, "you pounded." He went to the refrigerator, opened another beer, and held it out.

"Your mother told me that you're joining the air force," Applelow said. "Is that not the plan?"

Zach was looking at the pictures of Applelow's dead parents now. Of his sister, who'd asked him for financial help with their father's assisted-living costs, who'd called him a failure when he'd confessed he couldn't spare a dime. He hadn't spoken to her in the three years since.

"No," Zach said. "I mean, maybe. Between you and me," he lowered his voice, "I haven't actually joined yet. That's just the party line right now. It calms Mom down if she thinks I've got a clear direction."

"Gotcha."

"That's black hole, by the way."

"Black hole?"

"It's an expression my journalism teacher uses. It means 'that disappears,' i.e., Do not repeat that I haven't joined the air force."

"Understood," Applelow said, raising the beer. "Black hole."

"Plus not everyone's born with a clear direction. Mom doesn't get this, of course. Because of my brother."

"The famous Aaron."

"You've met little big bro?"

"He didn't live up to the hype," Applelow said.

This doubled Zach over. "That shit is *cold*," he said. They clinked cans again. "Kid's a freak." Zach finished his beer and opened another. "He had this, like, inner compass pointing north from age two. Me taking the crooked path makes Mom feel like she's fucked up somehow." He ran his hand through his buzzed hair, feeling his scalp. "I suffer the comparison."

The observation struck Applelow as dead-on. "Kid's a freak," he repeated.

"Yeah," Zach said, ruminating, "but a *smart* freak." He chugged his beer and burped, tapping his fist to his chest with such effortless cool it was an utterly un-Kastopolis gesture. "Gotta bounce, man. I'm beat. I'm gonna crash. It was good rapping with you." He held an open hand out wide, and when Applelow went to shake it, Zach pulled them together so their shoulders bumped, slapping his back bracingly and then releasing him from this hug. "Hey," he said at the door. "Can I ask you something?"

"Yeah?"

"My mom's all right, right?"

Applelow looked at the boy: his good looks, his odd confidence, his youth. Was I ever anything like him? he wondered. Was I ever as self-possessed? He imagined talking to Marnie later: he would tell her an abridged version of this conversation, black hole taken into account. He would paint a picture of her son that would reassure her.

"She'll be fine," he said.

Though he knew he was making a mistake, Applelow spent most of Tuesday and Wednesday by the phone, waiting for Ms. Samuel to call. But by Thursday afternoon, having heard nothing from her, he began to panic. He'd been wrong about the job. Taking stock of his situation, he pulled the book from its shelf and counted his money again, then gave himself a good dressing-down. After which his mood spiraled severely. He made a last-minute run to apply for work at some restaurants in the neighborhood, but almost all of them were getting ready for the dinner service; the managers told him to come back early the next day. He sat in his bedroom for the rest of the night in a fugue state, rocking on his bed in the pitch dark until he fell asleep.

It was brilliant outside when he woke up the next morning, amazed that he was still alive. Then he made coffee, cleaned up his apartment, and felt his spirits return. After a shower, he retrieved the Sunday classifieds from the trash and, committed to saving himself, began to read through them again, circling employment agencies and writing the numbers down. From here on out, he promised himself, he'd turn over every last stone and take whatever job he could find. There was no shame in surviving.

And then the phone rang. It was Madeline from Ms. Samuel's office, calling to schedule his return interview. He was so overcome with excitement that he asked her to hold for a moment, covered the receiver with his palm, and let out a long, happy howl. He pretended he had a conflict with the time she suggested on Monday and asked if there was anything available today. In fact, Madeline told him, something had just opened up and Ms. Samuel would look forward to seeing him at 1:30.

Which Applelow took to be a confirmation of what he already knew: the interview had gone well. Elated, he went to his closet and peeled the plastic from his dry-cleaned suit carefully, as if he were helping a delicate creature into a dangerous world. He picked out a shirt and tie and shoes and laid them on his bed. From here on out, he promised himself, he would never doubt his instincts again . . .

"David Applelow," Ms. Samuel said. "This is Dr. Pip Love-Wellman, our company's founder."

"It's a pleasure to meet you, Doctor." Applelow reached out to shake his hand, but the man steepled his fingers together and bowed slightly from the chest.

"Please, call me Love."

"Thank you," Applelow said, baffled, and took a seat.

"Or Pip, I don't mind Pip!"

Applelow looked at Ms. Samuel for encouragement. She, unfortunately, was looking at Love. Or Pip.

"It's short for Piper," the doctor said, and left it at that.

Applelow nodded at Love slowly, and then at Ms. Samuel, who now smiled at him. She was wearing a white pants suit whose white canvas belt had a big gold belt buckle that matched the bangles on her wrists and the enormous gold ankh brooch on her chest. Love, meanwhile, had on a green, one-piece jumpsuit full of pockets like a jet fighter's uniform, but with shoulder pads that gave the outfit an odd, futuristic look. His eyes were large, bugged-out, as if he were in a state of permanent amazement. He was bald except for gray shocks of hair above his ears, and like Ms. Samuel he wore a gold ankh pin on his lapel.

"Why don't we get started?" Love said.

Ms. Samuel, still beaming, recounted Applelow's professional history, highlighting different aspects of his résumé with perfect recall, stressing his strong track record of working with large groups.

"Wonderful," Love said repeatedly while she spoke. "Outstanding."

She ended by describing his six years with the theater company and how his abilities in diverse roles—as an "emotional multitasker" and "empathic alpha"—made him an ideal candidate for the position.

Love smiled at him warmly. "You were right, Ms. Samuel. I *am* impressed. David, may I ask you a question?"

"Of course."

"Do you believe in clairvoyance?"

Applelow was again taken aback. "How do you mean?"

"Strictly speaking," Love said, "clairvoyance is the ability to perceive things beyond the five senses." He looked at the ceiling and, with both his index fingers pointed up, made circles in the air.

"I see," Applelow said.

"But in our case," Love said, sitting forward and shaking his fist, "we're talking about acute intuitive *insight.*"

Chin in hand, Applelow considered the doctor's question seriously. "I'm open to it," he said.

"Outstanding," Love said. "Because at our company, we believe that everyone has a certain degree of untapped clairvoyant ability. An ability, that is, to read people's *auras.* Do you follow what I'm saying?"

Applelow, now in some despair, did his best not to look hopeless. "I think so," he said.

"Let me explain," Love said. "Every person, you see, has an aura which may be perceived as a color. That color gives us very specific information about their state of mind—even their *soul.* Now, with instruction, this ability to read auras can be heightened and developed to a point where it becomes a sense as acute as smell, touch, or taste. Do you have any idea how valuable such a skill would be, David?"

Applelow again looked at Ms. Samuel, who was listening to Love with an expression that could only be described as reverent. "Very valuable, I imagine."

"Try *very* very," Love said. "Think, for instance, of the practical applications. Think about airport security guards reading the auras of passengers at checkpoints. Or detectives reading the auras of suspects. Think about schoolteachers reading the auras of students, or doctors the auras of patients! Do you know what kind of world that would be, David?"

"A better one?" Applelow said.

"*Yes,*" Love said. "Better, safer, healthier."

"More harmonious," Applelow added.

The doctor smiled warmly and nodded. "David," Love said, "you continue to impress."

Applelow, thrilled, thought it best to nod humbly.

"But you don't believe in it, do you, David?"

"I'm sorry?"

"You're not completely sold on this concept of auras."

"It's somewhat new to me," he admitted.

"I respect your honesty," Love said. "So perhaps a demonstration is in order. Would you like one?"

"I would," Applelow said. "Yes, please."

"Wonderful," Love said. "Outstanding. Assuming you have no objections then, I'd like to read *your* aura."

Applelow looked at Ms. Samuel.

"Don't worry," she said.

"All right."

Love got up and stood to Applelow's left, steepling his fingers. "Close your eyes, please."

He closed them.

Love said, "Aaooommmmmm," and the sound, from deep within his diaphragm, began as a word but transformed, as he sustained the note, into a sonic environment, eclipsing Applelow's self-consciousness until this noise became a state of mind, trailing off as Love emptied his lungs of air and—as if they shared a body—Applelow inhaled deeply, his shoulders rising, and realized that he hadn't done this for as long as he could remember. A long silence hung in the room afterward.

"You may open your eyes," Love said.

Applelow obeyed, albeit slowly, in time to see the doctor sit down and sigh. He leaned forward and looked at Applelow intently.

"Your aura is blue," Love said, "which is excellent. Blue suggests expansiveness, depth, coolness under pressure. An ability to *flow* with things, like the rivers into the sea. Does that make sense to you, David?"

Applelow's mind was blank. "I've always wanted my ashes to be sprinkled over the ocean," he offered.

Love and Ms. Samuel looked at each other and smiled. "Outstanding," he said.

Applelow smiled too.

Love suddenly turned grave. "But your aura is blue tending toward black, David. I sense a growing hopelessness in you. An *anger*," he said, shaking his fist. "A *debilitating* anxiousness. Am I right?"

"Yes," Applelow said, amazed, rocked by the observation, unable for the moment to make eye contact with the man. "But I haven't always been like that."

"I believe you," Love said, reaching across the desk to touch his hand. "I do."

"Thank you," Applelow said.

"Excellent. We're almost done here. But there's a final part of the interview we need to get through. I won't beat around the bush, David. Succeeding here is critical to your candidacy. Are you ready?"

Applelow took a deep breath, prepared for any surprise.

"I'd like you to read Ms. Samuel's aura," Love said.

Stalling, Applelow pressed his hands together and touched fingers to his lips. "I'm not sure I understand."

"I want you to look at her, to focus on her, to trust your *instincts* with respect to her *essence,* and then tell me what color comes to mind."

"When?"

"Right now."

"But why?"

"To test your latent clairvoyant ability," Love said. "As a control, I've read her aura already and written its color on a piece of paper." He took a folder labeled *Auratec* off Ms. Samuel's desk and rested it on his knees.

"Can I prepare for a moment?"

"There is no preparation," Love said beatifically. "There is only *trust.* So please, close your eyes and begin."

Applelow, unable to swallow, held his fingers to his lips and stared at Ms. Samuel, who in spite of her odd outfit looked keenly beautiful. He closed his eyes and concentrated. Never doubt your instincts, he told himself, and named the first color that came to his mind. "Yellow?"

"You may open your eyes," Love said and withdrew the single sheet of paper from the folder, though he was smiling already: in block letters was the word YELLOW.

"Oh my God," Applelow said.

"Outstanding!" Love said.

Ms. Samuel clapped her hands once and laughed.

"It just came to me," Applelow said, laughing too.

"I don't think anyone's ever gotten it so fast," Ms. Samuel said.

"Now," Love said, "before our final interview, I want you to promise me you'll address yourself to your anger—this blackness that negates your blueness, this dark cloud floating over your pacific sea. *That* is your assignment. Can you do *that* for me, David?"

"There's going to be another interview?" Applelow said.

"Just one more," Love said. "I won't lie to you, David. We've had over one hundred and fifty applicants for this job. Perhaps it's because our base salary is so high. Perhaps it's the positive aura emanating from our company. But know this: of all of those applicants, only two others have made it to the final round. What I'm saying, David, is that your chances for success are *outstanding*."

He and Ms. Samuel stood up.

"If you're available," she said, "we'd like you to come in Monday morning."

"All right," Applelow said.

"Do you have any questions?" Love said.

"Actually, I do."

"Anything," Love said.

"What *is* the job exactly?"

Love grimaced, flashing his teeth. "We're not at that point yet," he said.

But when they did get to that point, Applelow thought, they would offer him the job in the same breath. Now in the subway, he stood at the back of the last car, leaning against the rear door and watching their progress out the window, the people on the platform and the station they'd left shrinking to miniature like something gazed through the wrong end of a telescope. He would start with Auratec immediately, perhaps that Tuesday. There would be a training period of some kind, but within a few weeks he'd be initiated into this arcane new skill. Was it really so hard to believe in? Didn't detectives occasionally turn to psychics? Hadn't the government recruited remote viewers to locate Russian missile silos during the Cold War? Applelow imagined himself traveling by plane to cities all over the country, Ms. Samuel by his side. They would sit together in first class and hash out tough problems; they would consult with large corporations and chair many important meetings. He'd work harder than he ever had! Within months he would've made himself invaluable to the company, rising to a position of prominence. He could see himself standing alone in a corner office, his hands clasped behind his back, staring out his windows at the skyline and the Hudson—a man who was professional, knowledgeable, who'd been saved . . .

As soon as he entered his building's foyer, he heard Marnie and Zach screaming at each other. Even in his bedroom he could hear them going at it, their voices muffled through the walls, their fight finally reaching a climax, when both of them started yelling with fury so private and unrestrained that it was as painful and repellent as it was impossible not to listen to. Then there was a thud, followed by a crash. The shouting ceased. Applelow went to his door and looked through the peephole. He heard Marnie moan, then saw Zach burst out of the apartment, pulling his coat on, his mother following right behind, taking him by the elbow. But he spun away, turned, and, bunching the shoulders of her sweater in his arms, slammed her up against the jamb, pinning her there. "Get away from me!" he said, and shook her once. "Do you understand? Get the fuck away from me!"

He shoved her once more and was gone. Through the peephole, Applelow watched Marnie watch the boy pound down the stairs, heard the door crash below, even his footfalls on the front steps outside—she listening as closely as he was. And all at once she slid down the jamb until she was sitting on the floor, crying into her palm. Because they were so close to each other and he feared being discovered, Applelow froze, his heart thudding, his fingers resting lightly on the door, and he didn't move for at least five minutes, when Marnie at last got up and staggered into her apartment.

He could still hear her crying when he left a while later to run a number of errands. As he hurried out, he passed Mrs. Gunther struggling upstairs with her groceries.

"Frizzing outsite," she said.

"Yes," Applelow said, then pushed through the door onto the street, where all was blackness and/or survival. Bills must be paid, and to do that he needed money orders, so the roll of rubber-banded cash in his pocket would be vastly reduced by the end of this trip.

Later that night, Zach showed up at his door, standing there with the hood of his sweatshirt up and his hands jammed in his front pockets.

"Can I watch TV here for a while?" he said.

"That's fine," Applelow said.

Zach slumped to the couch, stuck his feet out, and stared at the ceiling. "Mom and I had a throwdown," he said.

"Well, why don't you take off your coat?"

"I'm cold. I've been walking around all day."

"How about something warm, then? I have tea. Or coffee."

"No thanks."

"There's cocoa."

"What am I, three?"

"Is that a yes or a no?"

Zach turned to him, then looked back at the ceiling. Only his nose stuck out from under the hood. "Shit," he said.

At his small stove, Applelow poured milk instead of water into the dusty chocolate, then added sugar, a dash of cinnamon, a small chunk of butter, and a pinch of ground chipotle. A thin skin of white bubbles soon formed on the surface.

Zach blew on the mug after Applelow passed it to him, holding it in both hands while he sipped. "This is good," he said. In a few minutes he took off his hood, then his down jacket. He removed his shoes and pulled his feet up on the couch.

"Are you warming up?"

"I'm getting there," Zach said.

Applelow got him a blanket and threw it over his legs. That the boy took comfort in being here, that he himself was prolonging a cease-fire between mother and son, filled him with a sense of well-being, a secret optimism, as if this act of generosity was indirectly part of his assignment and would help him win the job. "How do you feel now?" he asked.

"Toasty," Zach said.

Psycho had just started on Turner Classics, and they both were quickly engrossed. Applelow hadn't seen the film in years, and now that he knew the ending the movie struck him as high camp, every frame with Bates in it a joke, every mirror he stood in front of and every line he uttered a hint at his doubleness, Hitchcock's genius more astounding than ever. Look at all the clues you missed, the director seemed to be saying. Meanwhile, Zach leaned forward on the couch, riveted.

"How am I gonna sleep now?" he said once it was over, and five minutes later he passed out.

Applelow put an extra blanket on the boy, then walked across the hall and knocked lightly on Marnie's door. She opened it wearing a heavy purple robe with the crest of the hotel where she worked stitched into the breast. Without makeup, her features seemed mannish, and she looked exhausted. "What do you want?"

"Zach's at my place."

She looked across the hall through his cracked door, considering the statement and his poker face with what little energy she had. "I'll come get him."

"No," Applelow said, lifting his hands, and to this she reacted with something like fear. "Let him stay. I don't mind."

She took one last look across the hall, or so it seemed, and pulled her robe over her chest. He expected her to be relieved at the news, perhaps enough to thank him, but instead her expression turned bitter.

"We had a fight," she said. "Did he tell you?"

"Not really."

"He didn't join the air force," she said, "and he's not going back to school. He wants to go to California now. Not with a plan. Not with a job. Just to go. I told him he would look back on this decision and regret it forever. I told him he was a fool."

Applelow offered no reaction, though inwardly he felt his confidence tumble. His father had said the same thing to him before he left St. Louis for New York.

"I told him I can't help him anymore," she said. "I just can't." She suddenly seemed defensive, as if she were waiting for Applelow to say something, though he had no idea what that might be. "So that's it."

They stood silently. He would've liked to take Marnie in his arms and hold her, not just because of Zach, but for himself. He couldn't remember the last time he'd so much as touched another person. She needed to be held, and he felt it might not be too forward; his own skin seemed to be pulling toward her. Is this what love felt like?

"I just wanted to let you know where he was," he offered, "in case you were worried."

Marnie shook her head sadly. Where she gripped her robe at her chest, her knuckles were white. "You think that because I know where he is, I'll be less worried?"

"No," he admitted.

"You can say that again. What's going to happen to that boy? He has no money, no education, no prospects. I can't take care of him. I've already spent everything I have to give him and his brother a chance. I have *nothing* left."

Applelow thought it best not to speak. He looked at the floor and saw that Marnie's toenail polish had chipped off in places.

"I don't even know what's going to happen to *me*." She seemed furious, and not only at Zach but also at him, for standing there at her door, which out of mercy or exhaustion she quietly closed.

. . .

And what, Applelow wondered to himself, is going to happen to you? He'd woken with a start, sensing someone else in the apartment—Zach, of course. The boy had gotten up to pee and once in the bathroom unleashed a steady stream that took so long to drain it was almost comical. He flushed and then switched off the light, banging into the coffee table and cursing sharply before climbing back on the couch, wrestling with the blankets and rearranging the comforter until he was finally still enough to fall asleep.

And Applelow suddenly realized why he felt such a kinship with the boy: They both only *reacted* to life. They lived only with a sense of what was right before them. If school pained Zach, he fled from it. If his mother argued his choices, he ran. If a few years' commitment to the military seemed like forever, he balked. Such a waste of time, Applelow thought. Such a terrible, enfeebling sickness that there must be a cure. He put his hands over his eyes in the dark. He'd spent his life accommodating himself to every occupation and situation as it presented itself, but with no thought to anything beyond that. As a copyeditor, he'd been conscientious and efficient, knew his style manuals cold as well as every obscure rule of usage from the difference between a two-em and a three-em dash to when to spell out an ordinal number, as if this attention to detail was accounted for somewhere and might somehow protect him. But when that job dissolved, he simply moved on to the next thing—enthusiastic, guileless, utterly malleable. He flushed away all of this information as if he'd never learned it, plunging along as if his future were somehow insured. When in fact, he realized now, his sense of the future was somehow impaired, and this explained the hideous situation in which he found himself. The future was as much of a blank slate to him—he'd come to see it as a kind of blackness—as his upcoming interview. That was his great failing. *This* was what was most cripplingly typical about his character. It was why he had no security, no job, no love, no children. His life fell all about him like a tree's leaves in autumn. Recognizing this, all he could do in response was urge himself on even harder. And the only thing he could take comfort in now was this odd belief—either a kind of faith or personal myth he'd always carried with him or simply a delusion—that something good was bound to happen. And it *is* happening, he told himself even now. It was almost like a prayer. He believed it, and this belief was like a beacon waving him on, and required nothing more of him than his conviction. If he got this job, he knew he would be confirmed in it. And if he didn't, then his deepest sense of life would be shattered. *That's* what was at stake. And he wasn't sure which would be more terrible: his defeat and ruin or the loss of this belief.

The next morning, Zach slept heavily through his host's alarm clock and coffee grinding, through *Morning Edition,* the news program dominated by the Iraqi prisoner-abuse scandal followed by a live report on the battle in Fallujah (volume turned up), until finally, at 10:30, Applelow shook him awake. The boy crossed his arms over his face, startled, then realized where he was.

"There's an extra toothbrush in the bathroom," Applelow said. "And a fresh towel. You can wash up here, or you can go over to your mother's."

The boy blinked twice. "I don't want to go over there," he said.

"I have to do a few errands," Applelow told him. "Either go over there or walk the streets."

Zach squinted at the bright windows. "It looks cold out."

"I imagine Alaska's worse."

The allusion didn't register for a moment, then he said, "If I come with you, can I hang here afterward?"

"Sooner or later, you're going to have to deal with your mother."

"I'd prefer to put that off," Zach said.

Applelow removed his glasses and pinched the bridge of his nose. He wished the boy was already gone; he wanted his place in order. But he remembered what Love had said about dealing with his anger, and he put his glasses back on. "Come along then," he said. "But keep in mind, this is important business."

Zach skipped the shower and brushed his teeth, but when he emerged from the bathroom in his baggy jeans, sweatshirt, and puffy down jacket, Applelow made him put on one of his overcoats.

"I feel old in this," the boy said, pulling at the lapels. When he saw Applelow's expression, he added, "I mean adult." Down on the street, they walked into the glaring April sunshine that gave no warmth, lowering their eyes and leaning into the stiff wind that gusted off the river.

"Where are we going?" Zach asked.

"First I need a haircut. Then I'm going to look for work."

"You mean like a job?"

"That's right."

He could tell there was an odd novelty to this that the boy relished: so this was how adults found work. They went to a barbershop on 48th Street, where Applelow had his hair trimmed while

Zach skimmed the magazines. Then he canvassed every restaurant in the neighborhood, Zach waiting outside while he filled out the applications (Availability: Immediately). At first the boy was patient, even curious, asking every time Applelow emerged, "How did it go?" or "Did you get the job?" or "What did they say?" But after an hour he grew impatient, distracted, and was dragging so annoyingly far behind that finally Applelow stopped at a market and bought him orange juice and a bagel.

"Is this all I get?" Zach said.

"I don't know. Do you have money to buy something else?"

The boy's face darkened, and he dawdled a good ten paces behind until he had to wait outside another restaurant. "Just so you know," Applelow made sure to tell the managers he was able to meet with, "I can do anything. I can host. I can wait tables. I can bartend. I've even done some cooking" (this last a lie). Most of them were kind—business was bad, they told him—but they'd keep his résumé on file. Others were openly dismissive, and at these moments he allowed himself to fantasize about a total success on Monday, the job offered on the spot, and this possibility fortified him. "Thank you for your time," Applelow told each one with an impregnable appreciativeness. Then, going out the door, he dreamed of stopping by for lunch next week with Ms. Samuel.

"Can we get some food now?" Zach said.

He sat slumped on an apartment stoop, head hung between his shoulders as if he'd just sprinted four hundred yards.

Applelow couldn't help but feel disappointed; he'd overestimated the boy's character, and now understood Marnie's concerns. "There's a pretzel man at the corner."

"I don't want a *pretzel*," Zach said. "I want *real* food. And I want to eat inside."

"Then go eat somewhere. We can meet at the apartment later."

"I can't," Zach said slowly, "because I don't have any money."

The street was busy. Applelow sat next to him and looked him in the eye. "And how does that feel?"

"What?"

"To have nothing. To have to ask a stranger for help?"

"You're not a stranger."

"No?"

"No."

"So what's my last name?"

The boy looked startled, then turned away. His teeth began to chatter. "I just want to eat," he said. "I don't want a lecture." He crossed his arms and stared straight ahead.

"All right," Applelow said. "We'll eat, and then we can go home."

"Thank you," Zach said, immediately brightening. He got up and started quickly down the sidewalk. "There's a Greek place I saw up the street."

At the restaurant, Zach ordered the dolmades (Twenty-two dollars! Applelow thought) and attacked it the minute the food arrived, shoveling it in his mouth and sitting back to chew between bites as he watched people walk by through the window. After finishing his stuffed cabbage, he filled his pita with rice and scarfed that down too. Then he pushed the plates back, slid down in his seat, and put his feet up on Applelow's side of the booth. He wiped his mouth dramatically, crumpled his napkin, and tossed a gentle hook shot that landed it in his water glass. "The crowd," he said, "goes wild."

Applelow pushed his soup bowl aside and, much to Zach's amazement, pulled another fresh hundred-dollar bill from his wad when the check arrived.

"What's up with all the coin?" Zach said.

Applelow shrugged. "I'm more comfortable when I have cash on hand."

"At least you're prepared for a rainy day."

He was so furious at the meal's cost he couldn't bring himself to look at the boy. "Yes, well, it's important to think about the future," he said.

The two of them sat quietly for a time, Zach flushed from eating so quickly, staring into space in what seemed like a trance. Applelow wanted to be rid of him, to have some time alone, but he recalled admonitions about anger. "So," he said, "what's next?"

"What do you mean?"

"For you. After this visit. What's your plan?"

Zach made a huge, cartoonish shrug and wiped his nose with the back of his hand, snorting. "I've got a friend in Los Angeles whose dad owns a painting company. They paint houses and shit. He said I could get a job there if I came out. So that's what I'm thinking. Might leave soon, on Monday or Tuesday."

"I liked the crab-fishing idea better."

"Yeah, but . . . I don't know. Where do you start?"

"By finishing school."

"Please."

"Get a job and save some money." He sounded just like his father, speaking in the paternal version of cliché. All of it true, of course.

"Since you bought me a good lunch, I'm pretending to listen."

"How will you get out there?"

"LA? I guess the bus. Do you know how long that'll take?"

"I mean how to pay for it."

"Mom will help me. She hates the idea, but she'll cave. She always does."

"Is that right?"

"Yup."

"Lucky you."

Zach pressed a finger to some spilled rice on the table, then flicked the grains away. "Never been to LA, though," he said. "I'll need to learn my way around. Probably need a car, too."

Applelow, now in a trance himself, watched people strolling by on the sidewalk. It was Saturday afternoon, the traffic on Seventh Avenue light, men and women singly or in pairs heading to a matinee, perhaps, or to nowhere in particular, Monday seeming so far off. What would *that* be like? he wondered, to have no pressing worries or obligations?

"Did *you* finish school?" Zach said.

"Excuse me?"

"College."

"Yes. In St. Louis. I'm from there."

The boy nodded. "St. Louis," he said. The place obviously meant nothing to him. "When did you come to New York?"

"When I was twenty-three. A little older than you."

Zach pressed more rice against his finger, rolling the grains into a small ball. He regarded this creation as if it were fascinating, then glanced up. "What was your first job?"

Applelow turned to the side, crossed his legs, and stared at the boy, who again was examining his rice ball. There was something animal in Zach's hesitance, he thought, a sense of random malignancy so strong it was almost palpable. Was this what Love meant by auras? Or his sensitivity to others an example of latent ability? He tried to detect a color emanating from the boy, but there was nothing.

"I was a park superintendent," he said at last.

"What's that?"

"I was employed by the city's park service to open and close a playground on the Upper West Side."

Zach appeared as impressed with this as he would've been if Applelow had just said he was an astronaut. "You serious?"

"Very."

"A park?"

"That's right. A park surrounded by a high fence, with a couple basketball courts and a baseball diamond painted on the concrete. There was a jungle gym and some swings, with black rubber safety mats beneath them. And a see-saw, too."

"So what did you do?"

"I told you. I opened and closed the park. I unlocked the gate in the morning, then sat down on one of the benches and watched the place. The park service gave me a tan uniform with a patch on the sleeve and a whistle to blow if I needed help or thought the kids were playing too rough. But I never did. Nothing ever happened there."

"And?"

"And what?"

"That was it?"

He cleared his throat. "They gave me a log to record the number of people who visited each day, and to list any repairs that needed to be made month to month. Also, I had to turn a sprinkler on at ten in the morning and turn it off at six, unless it was raining. I had a small office next to the bathrooms with a desk and a chair, and that's where I sat when the weather was bad."

He could see Zach picturing himself as a park superintendent, with the hours, days, and weeks passing by relentlessly.

"But what did you do all day?"

Applelow took off his glasses and cleaned them. The shame was making his head throb. "Mostly I read. I sat on the bench or sometimes in the office, though it got very hot in there. I packed a lunch every day and brought books I took out from the library and read from the moment I got there in the morning until I left at night. I don't think I've ever read so many books in my life."

"What kind of books?"

"Good books. Great ones, actually. Shakespeare, Conrad. Homer, Virgil. Austen and Chekhov, Brontë and Bellow." The boy was listening intently. "I had a notion that summer to read all the classics. The five-foot shelf." Putting his glasses back on, he could see Zach had no idea what he meant. "Have you ever read Shakespeare?"

"I don't like it."

"Well, I liked *him*. So much that I read all of it. *Romeo and Juliet. King Lear. The Merchant of Venice. Richard III. Richard II.*" He shook his finger at the boy, thinking of The Peanut Gallery's production. "Now there's a great play. Anyway, there was usually a terrific racket in that park, but when I was reading that summer I could concentrate better than I've ever been able to. It was uncanny, actually. It was like the words were life and death to me." Remembering, he spun his spoon around once, then looked at Zach. None of this was making any sense to him, though Applelow could tell he was still listening. "So after a few weeks, I got so involved with the reading that I stopped keeping my log. I just made the numbers up. Not that anyone checked. Which is my point. No one checked. Do you understand?"

"No."

"I had a free pass that summer," Applelow said. "I had *time*, and that's a rare opportunity. Like the one you have now. Because I could've been *doing* something for myself. Studying for the LSAT or becoming a CPA, even joining the military. I could've done something *practical*. Gotten something solid under my feet. No one ever does that for you." He shook his head, frustrated at his inarticulateness. "But it didn't occur to me. Do you understand?"

Zach stared at him, waiting. "No," he admitted.

Applelow steepled his fingers, rested his chin on his thumbs, and, after a moment, spread his hands wide. "I threw myself on the world." He watched Zach after he said this to see if it registered. He wanted to reach out and grab his hand or hold his face and make him look into his eyes until he admitted that he understood. But that would only scare everything Applelow had said straight out of his mind.

"So what happened?" Zach asked after a while.

"What do you mean?"

"With the job?"

"I quit," Applelow said. "I got tired of reading. It started to make me anxious—just *words, words, words*. One day I suddenly couldn't concentrate at all. I don't even know when it happened. I hit some kind of wall. It got so bad I couldn't bring myself to read another thing."

Zach nodded seriously. "I'm like that," he said.

"So one evening at the end of the summer I just left the park open and didn't go back. And I got paid for two months after that. It took them that long to figure out nobody was watching the place."

Zach's mouth dropped open at this. "That's awesome."

"No," Applelow said. "It was like being invisible. It was like not existing. I didn't even cash the checks."

"What?"

"I couldn't bring myself to." For a moment, he thought about this. He wished he had those checks now.

"But you got paid for doing nothing," Zach said.

"That's right."

"I want to get a job like that."

Applelow uncrossed his legs and turned to face him, folding his hands on the table and leaning forward. "If you're not careful," he said, "you will."

Back at Appelow's apartment, Zach changed his clothes, then nodded toward his mother's place across the hall. "The moment of truth," he said, and held out his hand. "Thanks for feeding me, for letting me sleep here, for rapping. Thanks . . . Applelow."

Laughing, David clenched his fist, which Zach appreciatively bumped with his own..

"I checked the name on the buzzer when we came in," Zach said, then let himself out.

Hearing him knock on Marnie's door, Applelow couldn't help looking through the peephole. The boy was hanging his head even before the door opened, and when his mother opened the door and regarded him, Applelow could see her react to his expression, mimicking it by turning down her mouth. Then she spread her arms and pulled him to her chest, kissing his hair.

"I'm sorry, Mom," he said. "I'm really sorry." At this, he felt something stir inside him, and he quietly slid the peephole closed.

He prayed on Sunday before going to bed. Though it made him self-conscious, he folded his hands and bowed his head and said in his mind: *Lord, please give me this job, whatever it is. Please, give me this job and I will work to improve myself. I will live from here on out in a straight line and never subject myself to uncertainty and promise You not to fail myself. I will work harder than I have ever in my life and will address all my weaknesses if You grant me this. Please, I have things to contribute if I could only break through to a place where I can. And I promise to if You will let me.*

Then he took the money down from the book on his shelf and counted it out. He had just over $1200 left, having spent less than ninety dollars this past week. He left two twenties in his wallet and replaced the rest. He got his coffee ready for the morning and set three alarms: his digital watch, his clock radio by the bed, and another in the kitchen just in case. He picked out his tie and spit-shined his shoes and hung the outfit on the door, imagining himself in it. Looking into the mirror he said, "So good to see you again, Doctor. Ms. Samuel, you look wonderful as always." He thought this struck the right note—someone who'd be a pleasure to work with. "I'm sorry?" he asked. "You were saying?"

The next morning, while he was shaving, Zach knocked on the door. Applelow greeted him with his face still lathered, wearing only the towel wrapped around his waist.

The boy had his down coat on and a duffel bag slung over his shoulder. "I'm catching a bus in a few minutes."

"Come in," Applelow said. "I'll be out in a second."

Zach sat down on the couch while he went back to the bathroom and, embarrassed by his flabbiness, closed the door.

"You got the suit out," Zach called. "Big interview?"

"The biggest," he answered. The clock radio was blaring away, and on the *Today* show Couric was interviewing a pair of amputee soldiers from Iraq, thanking them for their service and their sacrifice—and it occurred to him that this could become part of his morning ritual: the world's information streamed from dual sources, a quick check on the markets, the weather, the terrorist alerts. He would pick up the *Times* and the *Wall Street Journal* at the newsstand on the corner. What he didn't finish reading in the morning he would save for later in the evening.

"I came by to thank you," Zach said when Applelow emerged from the steaming room.

"You thanked me yesterday," Applelow told him, walking into the bedroom and closing the door so he could dress in front of the mirror hanging on the other side of it.

"I wanted to thank you for setting me straight," Zach called. "Seriously. I had a long talk with my mom."

Applelow had changed his mind about his shirt, and went for the blue one in his closet.

"She said you were right. I shouldn't just go and throw myself on the world like I was thinking."

"Good for you," Applelow barked at the door, wiping his hand over his forehead, still sweaty from the shower. It was warmer today, spring in the air, and he opened his window, letting the icy breeze cool him down before he put on the shirt.

"So I'm back to the military thing," Zach continued. "But *after* I finish college, so that I can do officer training. I'm going to commit to it, get something solid under my feet. See what it leads to."

"Outstanding," Applelow called. It was a joy to put on these clothes, he thought, his shirt starched enough to feel like chain mail, protective but soft. He got his tie right the first time, the knot snug and Windsor-fat and serious, the tip hanging to the middle of his belt like his father had taught him to do when he was a boy. He sat on the bed and pulled on his socks and shoes—the jacket could wait till last—and went into the living room. Zach was standing there, bag in hand.

"Good man," Applelow said. His sense of having helped the boy furthered his confidence about the interview. Blackness could negate blueness if you weren't careful, he thought, and by giving unconditionally to someone in need he'd also imparted his own best aspects to him: an ability to flow with things, instead of darting from place to place . . . and then he pressed his finger to his pursed lips and shook his head, suddenly understanding the point of Love's assignment so completely that he looked at Zach and laughed.

"So I'm gonna go now," the boy said. He seemed to want to say something more, then changed his mind. "So, seriously. Thanks."

"Thank you."

Zach started to back out of the room, then turned and opened the closet. "Wrong door," he said, laughing awkwardly as he hurried out and pounded down the stairs. Even over the radio and TV, Applelow could hear the front door slam shut.

He stared at the door for a moment, thinking about the next time he and Zach might see each other, and how much could have changed for the both of them by then. He imagined Zach in a military uniform, himself in a better suit. Then he went into his bedroom, put on his coat, stood in front of the mirror, and ran a palm over his lapels.

"Smile," he said.

When he arrived, a man and woman were seated in the waiting room having a conversation. Though the tone was cool between them, he marveled at how good-looking they both were, how young and confident. The man was tall and blond, with such fine, chiseled features that he could have been a soap-opera actor. He wore a yellow paisley tie and a dark-blue suit, and sat forward with his elbows on his knees, listening to the woman talk. Her hair in a tight bun, she wore a perfect gray suit and black, thick-rimmed glasses, and if she took them off and shook her hair out, he thought, she would be straight out of a dream.

He went up to Madeline's desk and said, "I have a ten o'clock appointment."

"If you have a seat, Mr. Applelow, she'll see you in a moment."

He gestured at the two people behind him and pointed to his watch. "I'm not late, am I?"

"Those two have already been interviewed."

He took a chair two down from the man, who looked over at him, nodded, and stood up. "Jeff Godfrey," he said, holding his hand out and shaking Applelow's firmly. His voice was deep.

The woman stood to greet him as well. "Elizabeth Myerson," she said.

They all sat quietly for a moment.

"Where was I?" she said to Godfrey.

"B-school."

"Right. You went to . . ."

"Wharton. You?"

"Kellogg."

Godfrey smiled. "I went to college at Northwestern."

"Really? What year did you graduate?"

"Ninety-nine," he said.

"Did you know Jason Meeks?"

"I don't think so."

"Don't you *love* Michigan?" she said.

Godfrey didn't respond to this, and Applelow, put off by his attitude, said, "It's a lovely state."

"Anyway," Myerson continued, "B-school was just so, well, unlike what I expected, you know? Maybe I was thinking an MBA would be more intellectually demanding, or I'd come out with a group of specific skill sets and so forth, but mostly it felt like a two-year corporate retreat with a whole lot of theory slash economics mixed in."

"Wharton wasn't like that at all," Godfrey said. "When I came out of there, I felt I could move into any area of management." Then he began talking in market terminology about Auratec's staffing needs and current revenue stream, how their expansion to the East Coast reflected their success in Los Angeles, Portland, and Arizona, shifting in his seat so as to include Applelow in the conversation.

But Applelow said nothing. Let them strut their credentials, he thought, because that wouldn't help. He was going to explain the outcome of his assignment to Love and Samuel by telling them how he'd helped change Zach's life. Communicating this was the key, he realized; it would distinguish him from these two business-school robots. He could almost see Love's beaming expression when he recounted what had happened, and his instinctive sense of the rightness of this approach almost made him want to stand up and shout.

"Mr. Applelow?" Madeline said. "Ms. Samuel will see you now."

When he stood up, the man and woman wished him good luck.

"You too," he said, then strode through the door.

He wasn't prepared for what he saw inside. But for two large black pedestals in each corner, on top of which sat large gold Buddha statues, all of the furniture had been removed from the office. The lights had been turned down, the shades were drawn, and Samuel and Love were sitting on the floor, their legs crossed, their hands resting on their knees, their middle fingers touched to thumbs in an Oriental A-OK, both wearing white jumpsuits with high shoulder pads that made them look like *Star Trek* conventioneers. Their expressions were beatific. Sitar chords played softly in the background. At the center of their half circle and lit from above by a lone track light was an enormous gold ankh.

"David," Love said. "it's so good to see you. Please, take off your shoes and join us."

Applelow, nearly undone by the scene, sat down on the floor and untied his shoes—an act, he realized, that invariably made you look unprofessional. He slid over to complete their circle and crossed his legs. "Like this?" he said.

"Perfect," Ms. Samuel said.

"David," Love said, his eyes widening, "you look radiant." He stretched out his hands and felt around, as if an invisible air bubble had surrounded Applelow. "Are you noticing this, Ms. Samuel?"

"I am."

"Your aura is exceptionally bright and in balance."

"Thank you," Applelow said.

"I sense, David, that you addressed some of the issues we spoke of during our last meeting."

"Oh, I did, Dr. Love," he said, floored once again by the man's empathetic powers, "and it was so successful that—"

"Wonderful," Love said, holding up a hand. "Outstanding. I'm anxious to hear about your progress. I won't lie to you, David. Hearing about people's spiritual development makes my job worthwhile. It's the ultimate perk, if you will. But we should get started immediately. Our two other candidates are waiting on your results. Are you ready?"

"I am," Applelow said, not sure he liked being hurried like this. He turned to look at Ms. Samuel for a sign, but she'd closed her eyes and seemed to be meditating.

"This will be a final test of your latent ability," Love said. "I'm going to be straight up, David. I won't beat around the bush. Get *all* the answers to our questions right, and the job is yours. It's that simple, and that difficult. Understand?"

"I do."

"Good. Now. Do you know what this symbol is that lies between us?"

"It's an ankh, isn't it?" Applelow said.

"Correct," Love said. "Outstanding. An Egyptian ankh. But do you know what it *symbolizes*?"

Applelow put a fist to his mouth. Of all the obvious things! "I don't," he admitted.

Ms. Samuel suddenly opened her eyes. "David," she said, "I'd have expected you to do *some* research about our company."

"That's all right," Love said, patting her knee lightly and then turning back to Applelow. "You don't have to be an Egyptologist to get a job with Auratec. Now," he continued, "the ankh represents eternal life—the force that flows through us and endures after we have passed, and that is imprinted in each one of us as uniquely as a fingerprint. Do you believe in eternal life, David?"

Applelow, fearing he'd done irreparable damage to his chances but sensing that honesty was imperative, spoke truthfully. "I do."

Ms. Samuel smiled.

"Wonderful," Love said. "Outstanding. You would have been eliminated from consideration if you didn't. Because we believe that all spiritual energy flows from the ankh. And it is to this energy alone that we train our employees to attune themselves."

"I see."

"I knew you would. We're now going to test your ability to read these different manifestations of the life force. To interpret, in sequence, a series of auras. Listen carefully. With the power of our minds, Ms. Samuel and I will telepathically project a color directly to your brain. You will tell us what color it is—just say it aloud the moment it comes to you—and then describe, in one word, what state of being that color represents. Do you understand?"

Applelow took a deep breath. "I think so."

"Outstanding," Love said. "Please, clear your mind."

"It's clear," Applelow said.

"Are you ready, Ms. Samuel?"

"I am, Doctor."

"Close your eyes, David, and we'll begin."

Over the sitar chords, he heard them both say, "Aaooommmm-mmm."

"Should I go now?" he asked.

"Yes," Love said.

As he concentrated, he felt a gentle heat at his temples, as if they'd been dabbed with Tiger Balm, and there came to him an image of his father walking with one of his building's tenants out the front door onto the strips of grass that ran along the walkway—a brilliant green in the bright sunlight—and then his father, as he did on the occasion of every new lease, put his arm around the renter and offered his help. "Anything you need," he'd say quietly, "anything at all, you only have to call me; it doesn't matter what time, just let me know." The memory was so vivid that he almost gasped.

"Green?" he ventured.

"Yes!" they both exclaimed.

"And what does green signify?" Love asked.

"Concern," he answered.

"Correct!" they said. "Aaooommmmmm."

"What do you see now, David?"

An image of Marnie's purple robe came brightly to mind, and Applelow felt his face flush. "Purple?" he said.

"Correct!" Love said.

"And what does that aura represent?" Ms. Samuel asked.

"Love," Applelow told her.

"You're right, David," she said breathlessly. "Excellent."

They both said, "Aaooommmmmm."

"And now?" Love said.

Applelow now saw Marnie's hair, an image from the other night when she stood at her door in her robe. "Red," he said.

"Remarkable!" Love said. "Representing?"

"Agitation," Applelow said.

"I won't lie to you, David. You've tied the number of correct answers of our third-best candidate. Continue."

"Aaooommmmmm."

In his mind, Applelow thought of bad nights when he lay awake in a darkness so complete that he couldn't see his hand in front of his face, and how he imagined hell might be just that: a lightless, morningless place and time that lasted forever, in which you were always alone. "Black," he said.

"Yes!" Love told him.

"Meaning hopelessness."

"Outstanding! Just one more to go, David. So focus! Pinch your concentration!"

Applelow felt his fingers trembling. "I'm ready."

"Aaooommmmmm."

And now he saw Zach standing at his door this morning, excited but also relieved and focused and ready. "Blue," he stated.

"Oh, David!" Ms. Samuel said.

"Which means pacific. *Calm.*"

"Yes!" Ms. Samuel said. "Yes!"

The music then stopped, and though his eyes were still closed, he could tell the lights were brightening.

"Rest now, David," Love said, and Applelow felt his hand touch his knee. "We're done."

He slowly opened his eyes. Love was smiling at him, shaking his head in amazement. Ms. Samuel, smiling as well, turned to look at the doctor, who nodded at her and said, "I'm speechless."

"Ditto," she confessed.

Applelow could barely contain himself. He felt sparks of energy crackling through him, as if he'd just leapt over some immense inner hurdle.

"Do you want to tell him?" Love asked Ms. Samuel.

"May I?"

Love steepled his fingers and bowed to her.

"Do you remember," she then said, "during our first interview, when we talked about how something good was coming to you?"

"I do," Applelow said.

"Well, it's come, David. We'd like to offer you the job."

"You would?"

"We would."

Relief washed over his entire body, from the crown of his head to the balls of his feet. "Oh, thank you," he said, and took her hand and squeezed it. "Thank you."

"Welcome to Auratec," Love said. He had his arm around Applelow now, as did Ms. Samuel, and they were squeezing his shoulders, and she smelled so beautiful.

"When do I start?" Applelow said.

After Love and Ms. Samuel exchanged glances, he said, "Today!"

They all laughed.

Ms. Samuel held up a hand. "There's just one more thing we need you to do."

"Anything," he said.

"Look over my shoulder," she told him, "just below that Buddha. Can you see anything?"

He squinted at something glinting in the light. "What is it?"

"It's a lens," she said.

"A lens?"

"You know what that means, don't you?"

"I have no idea," Applelow said.

"It means say hello to America, David, because you're on Fox's new hidden-camera show *Sucka Punch!*"

Suddenly people were streaming into the room through doors he hadn't noticed before that were on every wall—cameramen and sound people, a couple of producers, he guessed, and maybe the director, followed by the actors who'd played Love and Samuel and Myerson and Godfrey and Madeline. All of them were laughing so hard they were holding their stomachs, staggering toward him, shaking his hand, grabbing his shoulder, or slapping his back, roaring hysterically. It was a wrap! And Applelow laughed along with them, despising himself for it and pointing at the lens, with tears in his eyes, his face flushed with rage and shame, and it was cripplingly typical, he thought, that when he had the perfect moment to lash out, he did nothing but go along with the joke, as if none of this mattered at all.

"Oh, you should've *seen* yourself sitting there with your feet crossed," said Donald, who was still wearing Love's spacesuit. "You were concentrating so hard it was like you were in a fuckin' trance, man. Oh," he said, the tears streaming down his face, "will people do anything for a job, or what?"

That was the name of the segment, a producer named Ava explained: "Anything for a Job." She had a Fox News cap on, with her hair tied off in a ponytail and a set of headphones around her neck. "And it's the truth. I've got a woman in one gag doing push-ups for twenty minutes. But you, my friend, you're really something." The material was absolutely top-notch, and though she couldn't guarantee anything, the biggest sucker of the year would win $250,000, so he should sign the release—the producer handed him several pages of fine print—giving them the rights to the two previous interviews as well. "All taped," she explained, "from beginning to end." Applelow signed immediately, his hand shaking so hard he barely recognized the signature.

"Good man," Ava said, and slapped him on the back. Then a squawk came over a walkie-talkie. "Places everyone!" she announced.

"We've got another *applicant* on the way," Donald said, making quotation marks in the air. "And if she tops you, I think I might just die."

"It was nice to meet you," Ms. Samuel said, and waved sweetly. Her real name was Samantha.

The sound people and technicians were hurrying off the set. "We've got to get you out of here," Ava said, taking him by the elbow, "as in now."

Godfrey's hair and face were being touched up as they walked by. He gave Applelow a thumbs-up and said, "Great job, dude. Seriously priceless shit."

Applelow had nothing to say in response. After the producer showed him out, he walked dazedly to the elevator bank and watched the dial climb toward his floor. A woman in a suit dashed past him out of the car, her heels clicking sharply down the hall toward the fake office. "Going up," a passenger said to him, pointing above, and Applelow shook his head. When the door closed, he turned and watched the woman stop to check her appearance in the glass of a fire-extinguisher case, then pluck a piece of lint off her lapel and was gone.

He walked home in what he later realized was a state of shock, his mind filled with the recurring playback of people streaming into the room, their faces contorted with laughter, their outstretched hands grasping at him. At times he caught himself standing on the street corner after the light had changed, so mortified that he had to urge himself forward, and at one point he became so disoriented he wasn't sure how to proceed.

Then he turned onto his block and saw Mrs. Gunther at the top of the stoop, a black garbage bag in her hand. She took each step right foot first, and once at street level she threw her bag against the pile of trash and kicked it, slapping her hands together like a child who'd just completed a difficult task—or like a woman who no longer needed his help. He waited for her to enter the building before he walked up the rest of the block, and the sun came out as he stared up the steps. It was so bright when he entered the foyer that his eyes had to adjust for a moment to the dark stairwell, which he staggered up, the banister creaking as he clutched it, to his landing, where he stood staring at his keys. Outside, the wind gusted fiercely, shaking the door frame and rattling garbage-can lids. He heard a woman on the street say, "Oh, my!" and then laugh.

Marnie's door opened behind him. She was wearing a suit, dressed for work, with her hair and makeup done. Her eyes looked large and bright, and her teeth very white against her lipstick, though in the gloom he could barely make out any colors. But she seemed calm and happy, and she smiled at him without pretense. "I heard you come up the stairs," she said.

He looked down at the sunlit foyer, then at the keys in his hand.

"I wanted to thank you," she said. "For talking to Zach. For letting him stay with you. I don't know what you told him, but somehow you set him straight."

Applelow nodded.

"I didn't think he could be, but you did it. He left for school this morning, and he'll go into the military in the summer. It's been such a relief to me I can't even say."

Again he looked at his keys, as if they wouldn't work or he might jam the wrong one into the lock.

"Are you all right?" Marnie said.

"I'm fine."

"You look nice."

He glanced down at his tie. "Thank you."

"How about we have a drink this week?" she said. "My treat. You can stop by the hotel."

"All right," he said.

Marnie checked her watch and said, "God, I've got to finish getting ready," then raced back into her apartment.

Once inside, Applelow took off his coat, though he was cold to the bone. His message machine was blinking and he pressed *Play*: it was a restaurant manager from down the street calling to say he had an opening, that he'd appreciate hearing back from Applelow at his earliest convenience. In fact, if he was available this evening, he could start training immediately.

The bedroom door was open and he thought he might lie down, but it was so dark in there that it spooked him. He'd left the coffeemaker on, the stinking dregs burned to the bottom of the carafe. He rinsed it out and watched the brownish-black liquid swirl down the drain. Then he took his money from his wallet and pulled the book down from his shelf, and when he opened it a handwritten note fell from the pages and twirled to the floor.

APPLELOW, I PROMISE I WILL PAY YOU BACK WITH INTEREST A THOUSAND TIMES AFTER I LEARN MY WAY AROUND.

—ZACH

He replaced the book immediately, almost throwing it back on the shelf, as if it were scalding to the touch. Then he went through the whole process again, but the book was obviously empty. So he began pulling down book after book, flipping through the pages and finding each one empty. Finished but even more frantic, he ripped the whole shelf off the wall, then got down on his knees and started peeling off the bindings and tearing the loose pages into little pieces. If a book was too thick he wadded up the cover and threw it as hard as he could in whatever direction, until none were left, nothing more to destroy, and he kneeled there with his chest heaving.

"David?" Marnie called from the landing. "Are you all right?"

He grabbed Zach's note off the table and flung the door open so hard that it dented the wall.

Marnie, who'd raised her fist to knock again, stepped back in fright. "I heard noise," she said. She looked terrified. Applelow waited in the doorway, his shoulders pumping.

She took another half step back from him. "What is it?" she asked.

"Zach," he said, his chest still heaving. He held up the note, shook it, then took her hand and slapped the paper into her palm. "Your son," he said. "That *boy*."

"What?" she said. "What happened?" Her composure was crumbling before him, as if she suspected that whatever he was about to say would destroy it once and for all. Her eyes darted over the note as if she were experiencing REM. "I don't understand. What does this mean?"

Seeing her like this, Applelow couldn't speak for a moment: he simply didn't have the words, or how to enumerate her various failures. The landing was so dark that when he looked at her he could see only blacks and grays—and he was suddenly exhausted.

"David," she cried, her face sour with tears. "Say what you were going to! Tell me what this means!" She put a hand over her mouth.

"I wanted to say," Applelow began, watching her, "to *tell* you," he added, shaking a finger in the air and then pressing it to the note, "that Zach's . . . going to be *fine*." He opened his arms out wide. "You should know that," he said. "From *me*." He took off his glasses and wiped his forehead with the back of his hand. "I wanted to tell you that before, and I forgot. I just forgot to. So that's all."

Marnie waited for him to say something more, but when he didn't she laughed just once and wiped her eyes with the heels of her hands. "Thank you," she said. "I'm glad you think so." She laughed again, though it sounded like a sob. "I think he's going to be fine too." She took a handkerchief out of her purse and dabbed at her tears. "I'm sorry," she said. "You startled me."

"No, I'm sorry," he said, leaning against the jamb. "It's been an awful day." He watched her collect herself. "I didn't mean to scare you."

"That's all right," she said. "I scare pretty easily."

"I do too."

She handed back the note. "Well," she said. "I really have to go now."

"Good-bye, then," he said.

Standing at his door, he watched her walk down the flight of stairs. She took each step carefully, her fingers gliding lightly along the banister. It was so bright in the foyer that she seemed to be descending into a different realm, the square of sunlight downstairs every bit as white as the darkness in his bedroom was solidly black. Marnie's form was a mere silhouette on the stairs, but her color was restored at the bottom. Her suit, Applelow could see now, was a deep blue, her blouse purple, her hair red, her skin pale white. At the door, she stopped and took a pair of sunglasses from her purse—they had green lenses and gold frames—and put them on before she stepped outside. And when she did, her dark-blue overcoat billowed out behind her, the gusts whistling until the door closed gently and sealed off the sound.

Soon enough, Applelow thought, she would know some version of what he already knew. Soon enough, Zach would confess, and perhaps land back here. But not now. No, this was a different matter entirely. For now, he told himself, say nothing. Bring no suffering. Share no harm. He repeated these commandments over and over again, because these were the only things about his future that he could control.

The Rest of It

From the basement below Roddy Thane's office came a sudden clanging, then his radiator burbled and hissed. It was winter and the English department's boiler had been out for more than a week. A number of professors had brought in space heaters and several fuses had shorted out, damaging the building's wiring. So the college's head maintenance man, Mike Donato, had lately been ubiquitous. When Thane was leaving in the evenings he often saw Donato, grounding outlets in the hallway or staring up at the burnt, twisted guts of a ceiling fixture. Or he heard him working his mysteries in the basement, cursing the old boiler, his voice carried along the pipes and up into Thane's office as if through a tin-cup telephone.

Now the clanging reverberated through the building, a repeat concussion of metal to metal, followed by a sound like multiple kettles being put on a stove. It was Friday evening, almost 7:30. Everyone but Thane had gone home.

A few minutes later, Donato knocked on his door. "Have we got heat, Professor?"

Thane closed his tabloid magazine, clicked off the radio, and waved him inside. Donato, severely bowlegged, walked like he had a bishop's miter pinched between his thighs. He squatted in front of the radiator, turning its black knob to cut off the steam, twisting it again until it hissed back to life.

"Nice work," Thane said.

Donato shrugged. "This is just a patch-up job." He stood up, smacked his hands clean, and winked, then took off his glasses—a piece of electrical tape holding one of the hinges together—and wiped them clean on his shirttail. "To be honest, they'll need to spring for a new boiler."

Donato could have been fifty-two or sixty-two; it was difficult to tell. He was broad, his height mostly torso, with long arms that ended in monstrous hands. His white hair was cut razor short in a sort of tonsure that grew down from his sideburns to a thin beard and moustache, all of a piece. He had two duplicate rows of dotted scars down his neck, which looked to Thane like they'd been made with a cigarette. He was friendly and quick with a joke, almost roguish with the women of the department, secretaries and professors alike. They seemed to respond to something in his physical confidence, a comfort in his own skin that put them at ease—and Thane as well. He'd begun to dread going home, so they'd fallen into the habit of talking in the evenings. Tonight, Donato had already launched into one of his stories.

"And I hadn't had a lick of sailing experience before this job," he said.

"What year was this?" Thane asked.

"Eighty-one?" Donato was sitting across from Thane now.

"Maybe a couple of years later." He patted his chest pocket for his cigarettes. It was illegal to smoke in the building, but not to be left out, Thane cracked his window and lit up himself. "The guy I was first mate for, this army buddy of mine, Tuck Ralston, he owned this seventy-foot boat, the *Du-Tell,* that he used as a private charter. Took couples out for a week and sailed them up and down the Exuma islands or all around the Bahamas."

"That sounds like a good gig."

"Oh, yeah. So good you forgot you were in paradise. Ralston was into all this crap with the Cuban underground, so sometimes we'd smuggle cigars into Miami, small-time contraband like that up from Jamaica and the Dominican Republic, which wasn't hard because Ralston was down with the Coast Guard."

"Down how?"

"He went out of his way to help them if there was a distress call in our vicinity that they couldn't get to, or a boat that needed a tow. Let them know he was a good citizen. Especially if we were up around Andros Island or Bimini and heading toward Florida. They appreciated this, so they left us alone."

"Got it."

"Which is the story. I mean, how this thing happened. We'd just picked up all of this cocaine off Port-au-Prince—like a lot more than either of us was comfortable running—and were pretty jumpy about it. We're at sea, within a few days' sail of Miami, in the process of, I shit you not, packing kilos into the gaff-sail boom and rewelding it to the aftermast, when we get a call from the Coast Guard asking for a report on our position. And we're like, *Fuck.* What do *they* want? We'd come up through

Haiti hauling ass in perfect conditions and were about fifty miles west of Andros Island. We tell them our position and they say, Perfect, can you check in on this old woman who lives on a private island ten clicks to your north? Neither she nor the two servants she's got have answered radio calls. Coast Guard says they don't have the manpower right now to check it out for themselves, she's an American citizen in kind of a Bahamian jurisdiction, et cetera. So Ralston's like, Roger that, not a problem. Which in my mind was a *big* fucking problem. We've got ten years' worth of dope aboard, and I just want to get it off the boat, you know? But Ralston's policy was to help the Coast Guard no matter what, so we do it.

"The island's this small, off-the-máp place—there are dozens of cays like that down there—and it's maybe a half mile around. Big white stucco house you could see from the water. Red tile roof, a pen for livestock. Even a stable off the main house, but there's no horse, no nothing. The place looks completely deserted from offshore. And Ralston says to me, 'What we've got here,' he says, 'is an old lady dead of a heart attack or a robbery, and a couple of servants who bugged out.' Which seemed like a solid theory because there's not another boat in sight and it doesn't look like there's a soul around.

"So we anchor, launch the outboard, drag the Zodiac onto the beach, and head up to the main house. The front door's wide open, so we call out. No one answers. We walk into this huge great room, marble floors, beautiful furniture, a bazillion-dollar place. All the windows are open, curtains blowing, a small secretary's desk by the door with all the letters and correspondence and shit warped from the rain and scattered by the breeze. A couple lights are on, but there's no people."

"Nothing?"

"Zippo. The kitchen's immaculate, the fridge is cleaned out. The garbage can got knocked over, but there's no garbage in it to speak of—even the opened aluminum cans are clean. There are empty dog bowls, but no dogs. And no sign of a robbery. There's art on the wall, china on the mantel, a stereo, a television, even some cash in the secretary. It's like the fucking Bermuda Triangle. So we go upstairs to finish our sweep.

"And it's a total horror show up there. There are three bedrooms, and in each one there's been a fucking massacre. Like something you hear about in Africa, Hutu and Tutsi shit. The floors are covered with blood, the walls all sprayed with it. There are bloody handprints everywhere, bloody footprints on the floor. Psycho stuff. Like the victims had been liquefied. The beds are bloody, the sheets coagulated into crazy shapes. The furniture's all smashed up. But no bodies."

"I don't understand."

"We didn't either. We didn't know *what* to think. And it's the same thing when we check out the livestock. The chicken coop looks like a bomb went off, and there's not a carcass in sight. We find three goat's collars and bells in the pen—but no goats. The stable's covered in blood, like the horse blew up, but there's not so much as a hoof."

"So then what?"

"Game over. We're both so spooked Ralston's like, 'Marines, we are *leaving.*' We come out of the stable, checking our backs for whatever demon came flying through the place, when Ralston grabs my shoulder and points down the beach. And maybe a thousand yards away, we see these two black things just hauling ass at us. We can't make them out at first. There's glare and heat haze, and these things are rippling and elongated, tall as horses. They looked like they're made of smoke—coming so fast that we stand there and wait, like a couple of fucking morons, until they're within maybe three hundred yards.

"They're two enormous Dobermans. But it doesn't compute at first, you know? We're just fiddling with our dicks watching them run like we're at the dog track. Like, 'Look at 'em go!' And Ralston says to me, 'Sons of bitches must be hungry.' And I'm like, 'Yeah, they must be *starving*.' And I look at Ralston and he looks at me . . .

"And then it's a foot race. The lightbulbs go on in our heads and Ralston and I start *sprinting* to the Zodiac. We've got maybe seventy-five yards to the boat, the dogs two hundred to us, and we're all headed for a collision . . .

"We get to the raft first, shouldering it into the water like a blocking sled. The dogs *dive* in after us. I mean they *leap* into the sea full stretch—*pow!*—like those Labs you see on ESPN. They swim after us, ears back, chugging along. And they don't *stop* swimming until after we get the outboard going and *really* put some distance between us. And even after that, after we pull away and they swim back to shore and shake off, they sit down on the beach, calm as kings, and just watch us. Like maybe we'll change our minds and come back to be their dinner."

Donato started to laugh, coughing productively. Thane rocked back in pleasure, amazed. "So what happened?"

"So we called it in once we got back to the boat. The Coast Guard updated us a week later. Apparently the woman ran out of food, her radio was out, and the dogs turned on her and the servants. Ate everything. Most of the indigenous animals on the island too. Even the bones. And Ralston and I, after delivering, like, ten kilos of cocaine to Miami, we get a commendation from the Coast Guard for exemplary service."

The man seemed to have an endless supply of these stories. Thane didn't care if they were invented or exaggerated. They had the ring of truth. Of real experience. What Thane had learned of Donato's family history was just as colorful. He was Sicilian, his father Cosa Nostra in New York. Donato claimed to have run numbers for the Mob as a boy. "Nigger pool," he called it. "You're telling me you've never heard of the nigger pool?" He was constantly amazed at Thane's ignorance; he'd often pause to look around the office at some imaginary audience or sidekick, someone to acknowledge how little the professor knew about the world. He told Thane about his two tours of duty in Vietnam, missions with Special Forces in Khe Sanh and Quang Ngai, about his stints in prison after the war: one year in Tennessee for aggravated assault, four years' hard labor in Alabama for gun running. Surely the professor knew that the primary couriers of illegal firearms in this country were motorcycle gangs. No, he didn't know this. Like the Dobermans streaking down the beach, images from Donato's tales stayed with him long after the telling, and he found himself thinking about them on his dark drive home.

There was a chirping in the office, and Donato produced an impossibly small cell phone from his hip pocket. Thane checked his watch. It was almost nine o'clock.

"This is Mike," Donato said. He looked at Thane while he listened to the caller and pointed to the receiver, shaking his head and rolling his eyes. "Right. Right. *All right.* Slow down already."

Donato sat forward in his chair, resting his elbows on his knees while he scratched his forehead. "Where are you?" He looked at his watch. "Give me a few minutes." He flipped the phone closed and smiled at Thane warmly. "The weekend has started."

He stood up. Thane stood too.

"You should get out a little, Professor. All week I'm here, you're burning it at both ends."

Thane glanced at the copy of *Us Weekly* on his desk. "You have no idea."

Donato turned to leave.

"Hey, Mike?"

"Yo."

"We should do this again."

"We will."

"I mean we should organize this material."

Donato look puzzled. "What material?"

"Your stories."

Donato pointed to himself. "You mean my life?"

"We could make a book out of it."

Donato checked with his audience again, then smiled crookedly. "C'mon."

"I'm serious," Thane said. "This stuff is fascinating. Give it the right treatment and who knows?"

Donato processed this, squinting at Thane. "You'd really want to do that?"

"Think about it," Thane said.

Donato offered his hand, and they shook.

Later, driving home toward Troutville, Thane wondered how long the whole process might take—from interviews to transcription to manuscript, from editing to first printing. He and Donato would sit down weekly with a Dictaphone. He would organize the narrative as a series of tour de force chapters: "In New York." "In Vietnam." "In Great Inagua." He would call it *Tales of an Anonymous Life*. The book's effect would be like a man walking in place against a moving background, each setting supercharged with meaning, the protagonist surviving at ground level, unaware of his part in this larger American tapestry. He envisioned critical and commercial success, appearances on the talk circuit, interviews on NPR. It would be a chance to pay off debts and move back to New York, where he'd grown up, maybe start writing for one of the major magazines or get a job at a topflight university. He could feel the power of the project surge through him, like it had its own destiny.

He was proud of himself for being so opportunistic. His ex-wife, Ashley, would have been pleased too, having always encouraged him to write things that weren't just scholarly. Thane was suddenly seized by a vivid memory. He and Ashley were in their car, parked alongside a dozen others on a ferry, everyone facing forward during the dark bay crossing. They were headed from Boston to Long Island during one of Ashley's breaks from law school, and the two of them were arguing bitterly. He couldn't even remember now what they'd been fighting about. He'd been yelling so hard that his neck hurt. Ashley reached back to where the windshield met the corner of the dash—he wasn't sure at first what she was doing, but realized a second later it was to wind up—and then struck him across the face. The blow was quick, and much harder than he'd expected. He went silent, holding his hand to his cheek. Ashley pressed herself against her door and pulled her legs up, ready to kick him if necessary. She looked terrified and furious, and Thane was on the verge of retaliation until he noticed the couple in the next car over. They'd been watching this whole exchange, both of them wide-eyed, motionless, astonished, waiting to see what would happen next . . .

Instead of turning off the interstate, Thane took the next exit and headed for downtown.

He pulled into Billy's Ritz, a bar and restaurant that was always crowded on the weekends. When he'd started teaching at the university this past fall, the department had taken him there for dinner. Besides the refurbished hotel down the street, it was the only public place he'd been to in Roanoke. The bar was three-deep with patrons, and after Thane ordered a drink he tried to look like he was waiting for someone. He watched the basketball game that was on TV, nodding at the group of guys in front of him whenever they turned to high-five each other, everyone else also paired off, tripled off, grouped.

Standing behind them all, Thane quickly drank three whiskeys and finally approached the hostess. "Where's a good place to hear music?"

At Corned Beef & Co., a band played on a stage with its back to the front window, the red klieg lights shining down from the second-level balcony and casting the room aglow. The club was packed wall-to-wall with kids from Hampden-Sydney, Washington and Lee, Roanoke College, and with plenty of Thane's own students from Hollins. He felt out of place, absurdly old, but he ignored it, pushing forward to the bar and yelling for a beer. The music was terrible, unforgivingly loud. Then someone tapped his shoulder.

"Professor?"

It was Ramelle Foster, one of his seniors, a beautiful girl from South Carolina. She had the same eyes as Ashley, green and wide set, and a number of times during his seminar he'd caught her staring at him. He'd warned himself to be careful around her.

"You're *here*," she yelled over the music. She elbowed the girl next to her, nodding her head toward Thane.

"Indeed I am," he confirmed.

She indicated the band. "What do you think?"

"They're good."

"My cousin's the drummer."

Whenever Ramelle leaned toward him to talk, she squeezed his wrist lightly. There was a sweet, citrus smell on her breath. Thane had to put his ear close to her mouth to hear her over the music, and he could feel her words on his face.

"I've never seen you out before," she said.

"That's because I lead the life of a monk."

"Oh, please."

"I'm serious. Nothing but evenings of deep study, grading, and meditation."

"It sounds lonely."

"Profoundly."

She smiled at him. "Here, hold my beer."

Ramelle took the blond ringlets hanging loose around her face, pulled them back, and tied them off, watching him as she moved, and before Thane realized what he was doing, he took a sip from her bottle.

"Come with me while I smoke," she said.

The bouncer at the back door let them out into the parking lot. Thane lit her cigarette, then draped his jacket over her shoulders and put his scarf around her neck. Perhaps it was the comparative silence out there, or the awareness that they were completely alone now, but she abruptly became more formal with him, having lost her confidence, he guessed. She talked about his Gothic Lit seminar so self-consciously that he was enfeebled by regret. He wanted to talk about regular things, to forget he was a professor for a while, to leave this safe middle ground and get to the place where they were headed.

"Have you ever seen the star?" she asked.

"What star?"

"On Mill Mountain. The big star they light up every night." She rolled her eyes. "It's only, like, *fifty feet tall*."

"Oh, *that* star. I've always wondered about that thing." He was standing closer to her now. "Why's it up there?"

"Because *duh*," she said. "This is the *Star City*."

"Right, but did they put the star up there because this is the Star City? Or is it the Star City because of the star?"

"You know, I have no idea."

She laughed at this. He laughed with her, relieved. She stepped closer. Then she reached a hand out from under his blazer, took hold of his belt buckle, and gently pulled him toward her.

"So," she murmured, "how about I go inside and get my coat and things. And in the meantime you wait here like a good little monk, and then the two of us take a drive up there to see it."

Thane laughed once, his mouth dry, and leaned back. She pulled him toward her again. "You want to see the star, right?"

"Yes." He couldn't help it, he was whispering.

"Good. I *want* you to see it." She took off his blazer and handed it back to him, but left the scarf around her neck. "Don't go anywhere."

She tapped on the door and the bouncer opened it. With the red lights shining off the stage, the noise, and the smoky air wafting out, Thane felt like he was standing before a dragon's maw. The bouncer nodded at him, then let the metal door slam, muffling the sound coming from inside the club almost completely.

He stood in the parking lot, blowing smoke rings. A few minutes passed. He imagined the star on the mountain as clearly as if he'd spent many cold evenings bathed in its light. He closed his eyes and imagined himself lowering his mouth onto Ramelle's. He thought about what that might taste like, and everything that came afterward. Then he stamped out his cigarette and left.

Elliott Doyle, another professor in the English department, and his wife, Marcie, who taught at a nearby college in Lynchburg, owned the house Thane was living in. They were on sabbatical for the year, in Ireland until spring. Back in August, Doyle had been one of the few faculty members to make a sustained effort to welcome him on board, he and Marcie taking him out to dinner a few times, showing him around downtown Roanoke. They had him out to the house for brunch one Sunday afternoon—another in a series of magnanimous gestures that in suspicious moments Thane had come to believe were part of a setup. It was a spectacular day, and the drive from campus to Troutville was splendid. It was late August and still hot, but the leaves were just beginning to turn; and as Thane took in the beauty of the rural Virginia farmland, he thought about Ashley. The road leading to this house wound through hundreds of acres of cow pasture bordered on the horizon by mountains. When Thane pulled into the drive and saw Doyle and Marcie sitting on their porch swing, he mourned that he and Ashley hadn't made it to this point together. She had always loved such country.

"This is a beautiful place," he said as he got out of his car. The house was gigantic, a three-story redbrick foursquare situated on a hill. Several cats were lazing on the porch, and a fat English setter came bounding happily toward him, Elliott following behind. "If I lived here, I don't think I'd ever leave."

"Then don't," Doyle said, taking the bottle of wine Thane had brought and looking at the label.

"Oh, Elliott, for crying out loud," Marcie said. "At least let the man have a drink first."

"I'm serious," he said. "Stay while we're gone. Save your money and enjoy the place. Just pay the utilities and don't let any of our pets die."

With Ashley very much on his mind, Thane accepted the offer on the spot. He'd imagined her seeing the house someday—which was ridiculous, of course. But after a few months, he'd come to hate the place. He hadn't accounted for the isolation. Though Troutville was only thirty miles from campus, the drive was all on winding two-lane roads, poorly lit and treacherous in bad weather. Once he got home, there was no leaving again for the night. The cows in the nearby fields made the most remarkable sounds—an eerie slogging as they walked the pastures, followed by throaty, prehistoric groans. The setter, Seamus, didn't like Thane, or at least he didn't respond to his commands, didn't sit or stay or come, and he spent his days roaming outside—which Elliott and Marcie had strictly forbidden. Sometimes he showed up at the door covered in shit or mud or both, streaking the panes with slime as he scratched at the glass to be let in. Once he appeared on the porch with a cow's skull in his mouth, the prize still webbed with purple muscle and blood, and when Thane tried to take it away, the dog bit him on the hand. Thane went berserk, kicking Seamus right off the porch. He grabbed a log off the nearby pile and hurled it at the fleeing beast, cursing him insanely. Since that afternoon, he never once let him inside.

In the mornings, the mountains in the distance were beautiful, but in the evening, the pitch-black nights, trucks rumbled through them with gargling engines as loud as propeller planes. Their headlights winked on and off between the trees, their red and yellow marker lights running from tractor to semitrailer, outlining the rigs' twisting length as they hugged the dark curves, making it seem as if the vehicles themselves were in flight. He had underestimated, he realized, the difficulty of living in another person's home. But now he was committed. Trapped.

Sitting on the porch swing in Doyle's parka, with Doyle's

whiskey poured into one of Doyle's highball glasses, Thane shook his head and covered his eyes with his hand. Give him a million chances and he would never have guessed that he would end up here, in Nowhere, Virginia, living under another man's roof—though Ashley certainly wouldn't have been surprised. *Do you know what I hate about your profession?* she'd say. *The lack of control. You don't control where you work. You work wherever someone will take you. So you live in whatever place you can find. And once you find out where that is, you don't even get to choose if you stay. You get to wait six or seven years to find out if this place you never picked to begin with is where you're going to spend the rest of your life—or not. It's like your life's a big spin of the wheel. It's like you've chosen never to have a choice.*

Drunk and cold, Thane moved into the living room and turned on the television, idly surfing the channels with the sound muted and thinking about Ramelle, feeling the cold air of another near miss wash over him. The university had a strict policy about sexual relations with students, and he easily could've gotten himself fired. As it was, he felt embarrassed by his behavior and dreaded seeing the girl on Monday, fearing her reaction. Police strobes flashed on the screen, and mug shots of a male suspect, in profile and front view, with a phone number below them, to which Thane paid no mind. Images of a wreck on I-81, a minivan's entire front end accordioned, an indentation on the windshield where the driver's forehead must have hit the glass.

Thane turned off the set and picked up from the coffee table a stack of the Doyles' letters to each other. He'd discovered them in Elliott's study, idly snooping around one afternoon. The letters were dated and written in longhand, and once Thane started looking, he found them scattered in piles all over the house. It had taken him a few weeks to piece together their story, as he'd picked up somewhere in the middle: the purpose of Elliott's leave wasn't study or travel, but saving his marriage. He'd found more than a hundred pages so far. Which of them had initiated this correspondence? Did they actually mail these letters, or simply slide them under each other's door? With a scholar's attention to detail, Thane had catalogued the piles and mapped out a floor plan of the house, marking their location in each room, so he could return them to their original places come spring. But sometime last week he'd managed to lose the map.

So let me paint the picture for you, Elliott, let me show you what it's like to live with you when you're like this, when IT's got you in ITS grip. Because the most insidious thing about this disease is not that I never know when IT will take you. No, the most insidious thing about IT is that IT seems to come when I'm happiest, when I'm at my most hopeful, for us and for everything, for children someday, for all the bullshit everyone dreams of—as if IT can smell these things like blood. Say I've taught a great class or had a satisfying morning writing. Or I'm just excited to see you. I'm headed home thinking we'll drink some wine before dinner. There's good music on the radio and in my head I'm running through what we have in our refrigerator. I pull up the driveway and see your car parked, but all the lights in the house are off. And when I open the door, I can hear the television. I come in through the kitchen and see your dishes in the sink, the cereal bowl you used that morn-

ing, the orange juice carton left out, one of the cats licking the bar of butter. I call but you don't answer. I think: he's walking the dog, maybe. But then I come around the corner to the living room and Seamus is lying in the corner on his bed. He doesn't get up, just gazes at me sadly. And that's when I see you. You're sitting on the couch in the dark. You have a drink in your hand, you've changed into sweatpants already, your shoes are off, and you have that inert look in your eyes—it's somewhere between disorientation and exhaustion. I look at your thumbs first to see if they're bleeding, and they are, which means you've been feeding on yourself, biting your nail down to the meat and rather than trimming the hanging piece you've performed a trapped-animal's surgery on it, chewing off the whole pained part. "What's wrong?" I ask. "Are you all right?" "I'm fine," you say. I look around. The place is a disaster. You look around too, like you're seeing the room for the first time. And suddenly I'm furious with you for doing nothing, for not cleaning up, and at the same time it's clear you're suffering. (Though that's what makes me angry: the lassitude. The inertness. The way IT sits on you. Pins you down.) "Do you want me to make dinner?" I ask. "Is there something you'd like? Something I can get you? A drink maybe? I bought wine," I plead. And you look at me like I'm speaking Hindi. You appear almost offended and I feel like I've done something wrong. "No," you say, "not right now." "How about maybe later?" I ask. "No," you say. "I think I'll go to bed."

I watch you lumber upstairs and then try to collect myself— though honestly it's like you're dead. I came home to find you dead, maybe for tonight, maybe for a day, a week, a month. My happiness at seeing you is annihilated. Suddenly I'm so lonely and

hopeless that I'm scared. I attempt to fend off this terror by clean-
ing. I scrub all your dirty dishes by hand and then put them in the
dishwasher. I clean the oven, the sink, the microwave, behind the
toaster. I wipe down the countertops. I wash the pet bowls and mop
the kitchen. This takes an hour and calms me briefly, allowing me to
temporarily forget that you never rally from this, that you're down
for the count, so I start dinner. Food, I think, will do you good. I
go upstairs, hopeful. I knock on our bedroom door, and when you
don't answer I enter. You've got the lights off and a book lying open
on your chest. You're under the covers up to your neck, and the
TV's on. You're watching a movie: Mommie Dearest. *If the irony*
weren't so bald, I'd put it in a story or a poem, but I'd be criticized
for obviousness. So I get in bed. At least I can watch it with you.
Faye Dunaway is strangling her child. Which makes me think of
your father, of course, that son of a bitch, and all the stories you've
told me about him, all his impossible acts of cruelty, like when your
cat had a litter and he made you put the kittens in a pillowcase and
drown them all in the creek behind your house. All those things I
used to try to love out of you. I want to turn this off, for you not
to see this horrible scene, but oddly it seems to be comforting you.
There's even something resembling a smile on your face. And that's
when it's clear to me that I need to do one of two things:

I could flee. Pack the necessaries and go, get out forever—
though I can't imagine life without you.

Or I could go to your study, I think. Get one of the pistols.
Come back into the room and say, "Elliott, I love you. Do you
know I love you?" And if you say, "Yes, I know you love me. I love
you too," at that point—right at that moment those words are out of
your mouth—I put a bullet in your brain. I put you down.

.   .   .

For the better part of Saturday, Thane redoubled his efforts on a piece he'd been drafting for an academic journal on Robert Louis Stevenson entitled "The Gothic as Antidote" (*"The Gothic,"* he wrote, *"is a radical form of delimitation, a concoction as potent, as destabilizing and fantastic, as Dr. Jekyll's potion; a solution invented by the imagination that is a* solution *to the limitations of imagination"*). He was productive, focused, and the work seemed to relax him. But that night he found himself unable to ramp down, and stayed up so late watching television that he slept well into the next morning. He had a pile of papers to grade by Monday and a seminar to give the next evening. He was disciplined for the first few hours of the day, but turned on the television to watch a quarter or two of football, and the next thing he knew the whole afternoon had gotten away from him.

He began the week behind in everything. It was frigid outside, the mountains crusted with frost, and his car took over twenty minutes to start. In answer to his worst anxieties, the first student he saw walking toward him on campus was Ramelle. She was with a friend, and Thane fought the urge to lower his eyes when she passed him. But she said hello brightly, without implication, as if everything had been forgotten.

At his office, Thane found a note pinned to his door.

Got a great one for you professor! Impossible to elaborate in abreviable form! Call my cell to set up a time. 233-1211.

—Mike

He crumpled the note, stuffing it into his pocket immediately. Donato's enthusiasm for his idea embarrassed him now that his own interest had waned. He vowed to make himself scarce for the rest of the day, and to avoid Donato until he got the message.

But that evening, Mike knocked on Thane's door.

"Professor?" He stood there, slightly abashed, with a newspaper tucked under his arm.

"Come in," Thane said, trying to look even busier than he was.

Donato remained at the door, shifting his weight back and forth between his feet. He'd arrived in a pressed shirt and pants, as if they were now on a formal basis, and Thane flushed with shame. Donato pointed at the chair across from Thane's desk with the rolled-up newspaper. "Is this a bad time?"

"I have a seminar in an hour."

Donato sat down. "This won't take long."

Thane looked up from his papers.

Donato stuck his chin out, waiting. "Do you want to take notes or something?"

Thane tapped his temple with his pen. "It's all up here."

"All right." He cleared his throat. "I ever tell you about my friend Mick the Knife?"

Mick the Knife, Thane thought. Unbelievable. He considered his book idea and was hit with another wave of mortification. He shuffled papers on his desk. "I'm all ears."

"He's actually a cousin of mine. Second twice-removed or something. But in the family."

"Cosa Nostra," Thane said, pointing at him.

"That's right. He's been all over the country the past few years.

He was in Miami for a while. Dallas. He did time in Missouri. We've run into each other a few times but never really got together, and then on Friday he up and calls me."

"What does he do?"

"He's a hit man."

Thane looked at him, folded his hands on his desk, and smiled. "I hope he called long distance." He decided he had to keep his composure. To be impressed, of course, but not to react too strongly to anything he said.

"Unfortunately," Donato said, "he called from across town."

Thane leaned back in his chair and crossed his arms. Mafia hit men, gun running, death in the tropics. No, he thought, it would be foolish *not* to act on this, *not* to use Donato for these stories. Thane would have to schedule their first official meeting as soon as he had a clear stretch of time. He looked at his watch again.

"You'll like this story," Donato insisted, catching Thane's eyes coming up from his wrist. "Like I said, I hadn't spoken to Mick in a while, but then he calls me up—right here, on Friday, when I was in your office. So anyway, on the phone he's hysterical. He says, 'Mike, you gotta come quick.' I'm like, 'Slow down already.' He's like, 'Mike, life or fucking death.' He tells me he's at his house. I've got to come over now. What do I know, right? I tell him I'll be there ASAP. So I drive to the cross street and pull up, but I don't see anybody. I'm about to honk when Mick comes tearing out of the bushes with a shotgun. Then he dives into the car and lies down on the floor in the back."

Someone entered the hallway. It was Gerry, the department secretary. Thane saw her leave earlier, but she'd come back, probably having forgotten something. She greeted them both as she walked past, and after Donato said hello he got up and closed the door.

"And he says to me, 'Drive.' "

"So what did you do?"

"What did I do? The guy's got a loaded gun. And *he's* loaded on top of that—I can smell it on him—so I drive. He's got scratch marks on his face, five deep grooves on his cheek, the top of his eyelid's torn too, split down the middle, so even when he closes it I can still see his eye. So obviously this is a situation. I say, 'Mick, what the fuck happened to you?' And he says, 'Just keep driving.' And I say, 'Mick, unless you tell me what's going on, I'm pulling over.' And he says, 'I just shot my old lady.' "

"Jesus."

"That's what I said. So I'm like, 'What the hell do you want *me* to do about it?' He says, 'Get me to Frank's.' This Frank's a bookie, a local guy. 'Frank'll get me to a safe house.' " Donato shook his head sadly.

"So what happened at Frank's?"

"*Fuck* Frank. Guy's a piece of shit. I wouldn't take anybody in real trouble to Frank's."

"Did you turn him in?"

Donato looked around the room at his audience, then back at Thane in amazement. "Mick? No chance I'm turning him in."

"Well, how'd you handle it?"

"You're kidding, right?"

"No."

"I *am* handling it."

"I don't understand."

With a snort, Donato tossed the newspaper on the desk. "He's at my house right now."

An interval of time passed—certainly no more than five seconds—but it was unlike anything Thane had ever experienced in his life. He imagined it was something a hummingbird must feel: an awareness of moving with great rapidity while the surrounding world remains stuck in slow motion.

Donato flipped the Roanoke paper open and tapped the cover story. EX-CON KILLS WIFE IN BRUTAL SHOOTING. SUSPECT STILL AT LARGE. There was a police hotline to call if you had information and an inset mug shot of Mick "The Knife" Mancuso. He was a thin man with a long nose, black tousled hair, and a keloid scar on his chin in the shape of a Y—a face, Thane realized through his panic, he'd seen on television three nights ago.

"You seem upset," Donato said.

"No," Thane said, looking at him. Adrenaline thudded from his chest, making his fingertips tingle. "I'm okay."

Donato sat there smiling expectantly. "We've got a hell of a story here, don't we?"

Why has he told me this? Thane wondered. Is this some kind of test, like him trying to find out if I can keep a secret? If I'll believe the things he tells me? Or maybe it's innocent and he's just taking me up on my offer to listen, now that something's happened, and he can't process how bad it is. Or else it's the perfect imitation of innocence.

He scrutinized Donato's face, but it revealed nothing. He seemed to be waiting for a reaction, glancing back and forth between Thane's eyes and the newspaper.

For a moment, Thane allowed himself to appreciate the move Donato had made, if in fact he'd made one. Then, slowly, he said, "What if instead of going home right now, you stayed here, and the police showed up at your place? From an anonymous tip, say."

Donato screwed up his face and sat back in the chair, hands turned inward on his legs so his elbows pointed out wide, like a samurai. There was a hint of rage in his expression.

When someone knocked at the door, Thane and Donato looked at each other. After a pause, Donato got up, cracked it open, and peered out.

It was Gerry.

"Excuse me, Roddy," she said. "I'm sorry to interrupt. Mike, I can't get the steam heat to turn off in the main office. Can you fix things in there before I lock up?"

Donato told her he'd come right away, then closed the door and leaned against it. He took off his glasses, held them to the light, and cleaned them with a handkerchief. "I'll come back and tell you the rest of it," he said.

"I don't want to hear any more."

"How's that?"

"Christ, Mike, if I believe you—"

"You *don't* believe me?"

"You've put me in a horrible position."

Donato looked around the room again, stunned. "You want me to tell you stories, so I'm telling you my fucking stories. Did you think this was gonna be *Alice in Wonderland*?" When Thane made no response, he dropped his chin to his chest, closed his eyes, and shook his head. "Look, give me a minute." He pointed to the phone. "Just don't get any ideas."

After he left, Thane sat there looking at the newspaper. He had to do something, like call the hotline. He picked up the phone and began to dial but then heard Donato down the hall, laughing with Gerry. He hung up the phone and walked quietly to the door to listen, thinking he should go straight to the police. He sat down at his desk again and read the article from start to finish. He imagined driving to the precinct and telling an officer at the front desk, "I have information regarding the whereabouts of Mick Mancuso." He could demand protection, but what would that mean? Witness protection? And what if they don't offer anything? What might happen then? He was sure his life was over, that all normality had come to an end.

But if I do nothing? He imagined the woman's family members and friends waiting for news, grieving. He got up and paced the room. Shivering, he put on his blazer and crossed his arms.

Suddenly, Donato was back, sitting down and exhaling loudly.

Thane leaned against the windowsill. For a minute, they both stared silently at nothing.

Before heading out again, Gerry peeked in the office. "I see you've made friends."

The two men regarded each other.

"You boys have a pleasant evening," she said, and left for good.

"What now?" Thane asked.

"What do you mean?"

"What are you going to do with Mick?"

Donato looked tired, crestfallen, like he was the one who'd failed some kind of test. "I'm gonna take care of him," he said. "Keep him safe."

"For how long?"

"As long as he wants."

Thane was baffled.

"It's his call," Donato said. "That's the rule."

"But think of the trouble you could get into, Mike. Why risk it?"

Donato stared at him as if this observation was too outlandish to merit an answer. He sighed again. "Well, that's the long-term plan."

"What about for now?"

"Right this minute, he's hungry, so I'll get him something to eat." With great effort, he pressed himself up. "I'll let you know what happens." He wouldn't look Thane in the eye and seemed terribly disappointed.

Then, without ceremony or threat, he was gone.

As soon as Thane heard the building's front door close, he picked up the phone and called his ex-wife. There seemed something inevitable about this, as if everything lately had been pushing him toward it—his restlessness, his inability to concentrate, now these outrageous events. He was sure she was home; he could feel it. He still knew her number by heart; it filled him with bitterness to call it. While he was in graduate school in St. Louis, Ashley had refused to consider living in Manhattan. She always said she was a Tennessee girl; she'd be miserable so far away from home, from the mountains, especially if that meant living in an apartment the size of a closet. Besides, she was a lawyer, and for *her* to afford living in Manhattan—Ashley never said for them—she'd have to become a corporate attorney working ninety-hour weeks. But after they divorced and she moved back to Tennessee, she met a man at her new firm, married him within a year, and promptly relocated to Manhattan. Two years later, she had fraternal twins, a boy and a girl.

Of all the injustices Thane believed he'd suffered in their divorce, this was the worst. At times he dreamed of killing her: flying to New York, showing up at her door, and shooting her and her husband dead. Or else he'd fall to his knees and beg her to come back to him—something he always feared he'd do if he ever saw her in person again. Other times he fantasized about saving her life, a recurrent daydream that seized him almost weekly: she and her husband are being mugged, and Thane happens to come around the corner and interrupt it. There's a fight, and he's stabbed or shot, mortally wounded, bleeding to death on the street while he confesses his undying love. A boy's romantic dream so clichéd yet so powerful that he sometimes found himself drifting off midlecture thinking about it. Even now, as the phone rang, he longed for such an opportunity to say something pure to her. Some unalterable thing that would redeem their failed past, but still recognize it. Because Ashley's new life had wiped their old one out.

Her husband answered the phone.

"George?" Thane said, over the racket of children's voices in New York.

"Who's this?"

"It's Roddy."

Nothing.

"Roddy Thane."

"Oh," he said. "Right."

Now hearing Ashley in the background, he turned up the volume on the receiver and asked, "How are you?"

But George had already dropped the phone with a clatter. In spite of everything old and new alike, Thane was excited to speak with Ashley. It had been several years, and there was much to say.

"Who is it?" he heard her ask.

"It's Roddy," George said.

"What does he want?"

"*I* don't know," George said.

She took the phone and said, "Roddy," cooly, as her little girl screamed in the background.

"Is this a bad time?"

Ashley quieted the daughter down. "What does it sound like?"

He now heard the son screaming back at his sister. "How are the kids?" he asked, insanely thinking of them as his children, the ones he should've had with Ashley.

"You know, they're kids. Joy and work, work and joy." She covered the receiver and said something to the boy, then announced that she'd come back on by clearing her throat.

"I can imagine," Thane said.

Ashley waited. Thane waited back. He needed to tell her something, today or maybe later, no matter how hard she tried to avoid it. He could feel her considering this.

"What is it, Roddy?"

They still knew each other, after all. "Something happened to me," he said, "something serious. I need legal advice."

But she again covered the receiver and spoke sternly to the boy, who was complaining about something his sister had made him eat. Thane envisioned what Ashley would look like at this moment, still in her suit, just home from work, balancing it all.

"Go on," she said.

"It concerns something I've heard. Actually, that I've been *told*. But I'm afraid to tell you because I don't want to involve you."

"Then don't tell me."

This tone had been only a budding threat when they were together, but now it had matured. Here he was, emotional, on the edge, while she chose to stay above it, all calm and stoic. He didn't say a word.

"One second," she said, the strain palpable in her voice as the boy's complaints grew louder. She'd lifted him into her arms. "There," she said. "Go on."

Thane whispered now, cupping the receiver. "I've been told about a murder. A murderer, I mean. His whereabouts. It's all over the papers here. But the man who did it is still at large. But he's being helped."

"You're not making sense."

He took a deep breath. "A man I've become acquainted with claims to be giving shelter to this criminal. A suspected murderer. At his house, right now."

Ashley cleared her throat again. "This isn't some kind of joke, is it?"

94

"Do I sound like it?"

"Do you believe this guy?"

"Given his background, I think he might be telling the truth."

"But do you *believe* him?"

"I don't know."

The little girl's screams made Thane jump.

"Jason!" Ashley yelled. "*Never* throw things at your sister!"

"I *hate* salt," the boy blurted.

"What are you asking me, Roddy?"

"What I want to know . . ." He took a deep breath. "What I need to figure out before I do anything . . ." He looked up at the ceiling and draped his arm over his eyes. This reminded him of all the long conversations they had after she'd first left, when he felt his grip on her slipping, their time together ending, but he wanted to hold her attention for as long as possible, no matter how bitter the discussion. "Is this aiding and abetting?" he asked. "I mean legally, what's my responsibility here? Do I have to call the police, or turn this guy in? Ashley, I don't know what to do."

She was silent for a moment, then laughed. "Oh, no," she said. "Jesus, Roddy, you actually had me worried for a second." She let out a loud guffaw. "No, it's hardly aiding and abetting. There's not a court in the country that would convict you for doing nothing."

"Are you sure about that?"

"Think about it. You've got secondhand knowledge you'd never believe in the first place about a crime that's been committed. And this man you're talking about could just as well be some psycho you passed on the street. Are you sure this friend of yours isn't crazy?"

Thane let her suggestion pass without comment.

"No," she said. "You have no responsibility at all."

"But what if this person commits another act of violence?"

"Who? This figment fugitive this other character's hiding? What if he does?"

"*Exactly.*"

"That's a moral question. And it's not really what you're asking, is it?"

Thane listened to himself breathe.

"Trust me, Roddy, you're safe."

They were quiet again.

"Tell me something, though. Why did you get involved with a guy like this in the first place?"

He thought about his book idea, then closed his eyes. "It just happened. Why?"

"Because it's surprising."

"What do you mean?"

"It just isn't your speed."

"And how's that?"

"It's kind of dangerous."

"I don't understand."

She sighed, and he thought he could detect a hint of fondness in it.

"Remember, Roddy, when we lived in St. Louis? In that little apartment of yours. Where was it? Dogtown, right?"

"On Clayton."

"We used to hear gunfire at night, that *clap-clap* sound. The DA I was working for and I both told you that sooner or later the person firing that gun would eventually find his way to my desk. And you said you never could do what I do. You'd never go there."

"Yes," he said, and heard the little girl say, "Pick me up too."

"Hold the phone for me then, up to my ear," Ashley told her.

He could hear Ashley breathing hard as she lifted the second child—a sound from deep within her he'd heard so many times he was shocked by how familiar it was.

"Who's that?" the boy asked.

"A person I know," Ashley said.

"Who?"

"Just someone."

"Is he your friend?"

"Maybe I should go," Thane said.

"Look, don't worry about it."

"Thanks."

"It's probably just a story."

"Absolutely."

"Everything else good?"

"Good. Great job in Roanoke. Beautiful house in the mountains. You?"

"Good." She set her children down, and they scrambled off. "Busy." The boy screamed again. "Life."

"I know what you mean."

"Take care," she said. "And Roddy?"

"Yeah?"

"Don't go there, okay?" She was referring to the incident, though he knew she really meant something else altogether.

"Good-bye," he said.

. . .

After their conversation, he sat staring at the telephone. Finally, after a period of time he couldn't measure, he grabbed his car keys and left the office.

He taped a note on the classroom door saying the seminar was canceled, then got in his car and drove downtown, having no idea where he was going or why. Downtown was only ten miles from the university, but there was a wreck on the interstate and he was stuck in traffic, just another vehicle in a long line of taillights inching forward, of tailpipes blowing steam into the air, stop-starting by inches toward whatever destruction lay ahead for them to slow down and gaze upon. Then everything came to a complete halt. Thane sat in the endless line with his foot on the brake until he grew tired and put the car in park. Drivers were getting out of their cars to look, a few even sitting on their hoods, their bodies blanched of color from the headlights behind them. Thane opened his own door for a moment but didn't unbuckle his seat belt, just looked at the road and, for reasons he didn't understand, reached down to touch the pavement: it was cold. Then he closed the door and cut the ignition. To his right was a family of four, two little girls in back watching separate screens attached to the back of their parents' headrests, their faces ablaze with cartoons. Their father's hands were fixed on the wheel in a pantomime of driving, his wife's face illuminated by the ghostly light from her PDA. To Thane's left, a woman in a business suit was painting her nails. He heard a roar and saw her look up as a Life Flight helicopter passed directly overhead, so low that the drivers standing on the road ducked and winced, their clothes rippling with the rotors' spill. The craft shrank quickly into the distance and soon all was silent again. "No good news arrives by helicopter," a doctor friend had once told him, and he thought of what Ashley had said—"Don't go there"—and then remembered Donato's note in his pocket. He imagined calling him, threatening to alert the police if he didn't let him come by immediately. He wanted to see the man Donato was protecting, to stand before him, to smell his fear, to hear what he had to say, if only to make sure he was real. Thane put the car in drive, looked at the median to his left, and saw he could make a U-turn out of this mess. It would mean something, wouldn't it? To break from his character, his story. To seize something. And he wondered: Was the old wisdom true? If you entered the dragon's lair, challenged and defeated the beast, were all its riches then yours? Or was there a succession of beasts, of one battle after another with no final outcome, no rest between victories? Because the world seemed too wide, its fortunes too random, and its blessings too fleeting to honor one man's bravery—or to punish his cowardice. Yet in the end, something must be done.

The Suicide Room

We were sitting on the floor of Will's dorm room, smoking pot, when the conversation turned to death.

"My sister, Elise, saw her boyfriend get killed in a car wreck," Casey said. She exhaled contemplatively, blowing a stream of smoke toward the lit end of the joint, which she held like a cigarette. "They'd left this party together. But they were in separate cars. And . . . what was his name—Doug! He was driving behind her. He had all these kids from the party piled in his dad's Mustang. Apparently he wasn't drunk or anything, but they were driving on this winding road along the coast near our house, and the next thing Elise sees in the rearview mirror is the Mustang crashing through the guardrail and going over the cliff."

"She saw this?" Alyssa said.

Casey passed her the joint and she took a hit even though she didn't like pot. Casey and Will were both seniors; they'd been a couple since the dawn of time. I was going to break up with Alyssa that night, but she didn't know it yet. It was 1986, and we'd just started our sophomore year.

"Just like I said, she saw them go over the cliff. That was it."

"Did the other kids in the car die?"

I couldn't tell if Alyssa was really taken with the story, or just trying to feign deep concern to a girl higher up on the social ladder.

"Yes," Casey said. "And no. Including Dave, the boyfriend, there were five kids in the car, and three of them died, one ended up a paraplegic, and the fifth, who wasn't wearing a seat belt, got thrown from the car and hooked on a branch. He hung there like a cartoon character until the fire department came."

"You're full of shit," Will said.

Casey shot him a look. "I'm *not* full of shit." They already communicated like an eternally married couple, their expressions registering with each other as clearly as if they were telepathic. "This was a legendary tragedy in my high school and a defining moment in my sister's life."

"There's no such thing as a defining moment," Will said. "We invent defining moments."

"Well, aren't you a fucking philosopher."

"How come I've never heard this story before? How did this one escape me?"

"Maybe you weren't listening. You never listen." She burst out laughing. We all did, then stared at one another's feet.

"I don't know anyone personally who's died," Alyssa said after a while. "Not that I'm rushing to have that experience." She was part Lebanese and had short dark hair, olive-colored skin, and enormous brown eyes—just heart-stoppingly beautiful. Occasionally I caught Will looking at her, enthralled, and it pleased me. She was trophy-pretty and just as smart as hell, and there was a feeling of one-upmanship in his admiration of her that I couldn't help but enjoy.

"But my brother was born with the umbilical cord wrapped around his neck and it caused severe brain damage, so I guess he's kind of dead."

Alyssa considered her brother for a moment. She had that far-off look you don't realize you get when you're stoned. I thought she might even cry, though she was rarely sentimental about Danny. I personally found him frightening, and not at all worthy of tears.

I'd met him this past summer—though you don't meet Danny so much as see him—when I'd spent the weekend with Alyssa at her house, ostensibly to take care of her younger sister and brother while her parents went out of town, but really so we could fuck every free minute that we had. Danny was the eldest sibling and very tall, easily six foot two. He was olive-skinned like his sisters, but slack-looking in the eyes. We all stood in the kitchen together while Alyssa's mother laid down the law for the weekend, and Alyssa's father, who was a plaintiffs' attorney for Vietnam veterans and scary rich, was standing with Danny and me by the padlocked kitchen cabinets. (Even the refrigerator had a digital keypad.) Danny was shifting his weight back and forth and watching his father the way a dog watches someone eat, which Mr. Richardson eventually noticed.

"You want some cereal?" he asked Danny.

Alyssa's father stood with his hands in his pockets, look-ing at his son warmly, almost proudly. There was an element of self-consciousness to the whole display, and I observed it carefully, because I enjoy moments when people think they're fooling me.

To his father's question, Danny made a happy grunt like, *Gyah.*
"Let's get you some cereal, kid."

Mr. Richardson unlocked the top cabinet, where the cereal was
kept, right in front of Danny, who obviously couldn't remember
the combination, and in front of me, of course, as if to demonstrate that no matter how brutally retarded his son was, the two
of them could communicate man-to-man, as if asking him if he'd
like a bowl of Crunchberries was like going to a bar together to
knock back a few beers. I thought the whole performance was sad,
and though I listened attentively while Mr. Richardson showed me
where the combinations for the locks were kept—literally every
cabinet was padlocked—perhaps I appeared intimidated by the
whole thing, because Alyssa gently pressed her hand on my back
and whispered for me not to worry, that she'd handle feeding her
brother.

The next morning I went to the kitchen to get some orange
juice, and when I closed the refrigerator door Danny was standing there looking down at me, as naked as the day he was born
and scaring me silly. Danny gave an amazed laugh, and pointed
at the juice—"Joos," he said, "Joos"—and then went for it with
both hands, wiggling his fingers delightedly. He took the carton
out of my terrified grasp and proceeded to drink the whole gal-
lon, the liquid running down the sides of his mouth. He was like a
giant goldfish, I realized. The padlocked cabinets suddenly made
sense; they were there to protect him from blowing himself up. He
finished and looked at me and said, "Ahhhhh," then burped wetly,
handed the empty carton back, and peered over my shoulder into
the lit shelves, but I'd managed to lock the door before he could

raid anything else. Needless to say, I got the hell out of there as fast as I could.

"That doesn't count as a death," I told Alyssa.

"We mean death in the pornographic sense," said Casey.

"As in eyewitnessed," Will said.

"I saw my grandfather get killed," I offered.

"No," Alyssa said.

I nodded. "He was a big cigar smoker. Loved to smoke them while he golfed, read the paper, took a shit. I smell cigars and I think of him. It's Pavlovian. Anyway, two years ago, he was eighty-four and healthy as a horse and then he went to light a cigar in his work-shop—he made his own golf clubs—and the lighter blew up in his face."

"What?" Will said.

"Blew up. Apparently he'd filled it with the wrong fluid and it was explosive. I came down to his workshop just by chance after-ward and he was rolling on the floor trying to put himself out."

"Shut *up*," Casey said. She was thin in the face and flat-chested and liked to reach out and touch the people she was talking with—she had my forearm in her hands at that very moment. She was so confident in her sexuality, so sure of how she took hold of you or pulled you toward her, she was like a full-grown woman. We'd been fucking for a few weeks now, unbeknownst to Will or Alyssa. This all seemed dangerous and delightful to me at the time, and so far as I was concerned none of this sneaking around had any real moral weight.

"So what happened?" Alyssa said. She began rubbing my neck while Casey still had my arm in her hands and was giving me a delicious Indian burn. I wanted Will to disappear, or fall unconscious.

"I put him out. But I made this terrible mistake, though I didn't know it was at the time. I threw my shirt over his face to snuff out the flames, and his skin stuck to the fabric."

Will winced. Both girls stopped cold.

I affected a faraway look. Not indifferent, more transfixed. "By then, my grandmother had come downstairs and had seen what was happening, and called 911. The medics came. It was totally insane. Anyway, he suffered third-degree burns on his neck and face and died of an infection a few days later."

This elicited a stunned silence. Finally, Will said, "I don't think I can top that."

"*Top it?*" Casey said. "Are you *sick?* This is his *grandfather.*"

"It's all right. I'm okay with it. He lived a good life."

"You were so brave," Alyssa said.

I was lying through my teeth, of course. My grandfather loved golf but hated cigars, and he was still very much alive. I'd heard this story from a high school friend over the summer and thought it was remarkable, so I'd adopted it and given it wings—I added the bit about the shirt—and told it every chance I got. It conferred on me, I thought, a bizarre sort of glamour.

"My personal and only witnessed-death story," Will jumped in, "was my uncle Nick's, who, I should add, I didn't like. He had lung cancer and it spread everywhere, though in spite of this he kept busy dying for what seemed like, I don't know, a year. Toward the end, there was this big family gathering—he was my mother's brother—out at his house in Seattle, which so far as I could figure out as a kid was a wait-around-for-Uncle-Nick-to-die party. I mean this literally. That's why I thought we were there. There were flowers everywhere and even a casket in the dining room, which at one point Uncle Nick went to lie in just to get the feel of it, and *that* was a strange thing to see. But I thought this was kind of the opposite of a birthday party and that at some point, just like the cake coming out, the guy was eventually going to sign off. I was seven years old and the concept of death only made sense to me as a very long trip you took, somewhere remote and possibly even fun, in spite of all the grief I'd been seeing, so I was actually pretty excited. For the party my uncle's hospital bed had been moved into the living room and there were people everywhere, drinking, eating, talking. He'd been on the verge of croaking for so many months I guess nobody felt like it should interfere with a good time. Anyway, after what seems like so long I can barely contain myself, my mother comes up to me crying and says, 'Will, it's time to say good-bye to Uncle Nick.' And because it was time for *me* to say good-bye, and because kids always think they're the center of the universe, I thought he was going to die *right then*—and that I was somehow holding everything up. So I hurry over to his bed-side. The guy had so many tubes coming out of him he looked like he was lying in a plastic hammock. I'm sitting there pumping my leg and he's staring at the ceiling, and I don't know what to do. I don't know if I'm supposed to sing some song or say a magic word, so I wait as patiently as I can until he finally notices me and says, 'Who are you?' 'I'm Will,' I say. 'That means nothing to me,' he says. 'Be more specific.' 'You're my uncle,' I say. 'I'm your sister's son.' 'Which sister?' 'Jenny.' He says, 'Oh.' Then he looks up at the ceiling again and says, 'My death doesn't belong to me. That's the thing about dying slowly. You're not dead yet, but people are already fitting your last rites into their schedule. You can see it in their eyes. *This might be the last time I see him.* There's no dignity in that. Do you understand?' 'No,' I say. 'No? Well, let's make it simple. Try to die quick. Not soon, but quick. Get it?' 'Yes, sir.' He doesn't speak for a while and I start to get anxious again because I still don't know what to do, but then he looks at me and goes, 'Do you want to know what pains me most about my life? The thing I regret most?' I'm like, 'Sir?' 'The women I could've fucked,' he says, 'but didn't. It's all I think about. I lie here, start chronologically, and go back as far as sixth grade to some time as recent as last year, thinking about all the opportunities for pussy that I didn't take, and it makes me want to cry. Do you like girls?' 'No,' I say. 'Well, I did. I *do.* And I should have fondled Milly Bear's fat tits before I met your aunt Carol. I should've squeezed Liz Coleman's ass and sucked Kathy Koch's nipples. But I didn't because I was afraid. Know why?' 'No.' 'Because I thought it *meant* something not to. That holding myself back registered somewhere. But it means *nothing* not to. It doesn't register *anywhere.* I want you to remember that. Tell me you'll remember.' 'I will.' 'Good,' he says. 'Someone is spared.' Then he puts his hands over his eyes and lays there mumbling these women's names, and I can't stand it because I'm not only getting bored with the Q & A, but also tired of waiting for the main event. So I say, 'Uncle, can I ask you something?' And then he coughs really hard for a while and finally gasps, 'Go ahead.' And I say, 'Are you going to die now?' And he looks at the ceiling and says, 'Yes, now I'm going to die.' Then he made a sound like a tire deflating, and boom, I swear to God, my aunt Carol keels over right behind us, dead of a massive aneurysm."

For some reason, this story just killed me—I was sure Will meant it to be funny—and I laughed so hard I went fetal. The guy could string me out from the get-go and then pull me back in at his leisure, and this was the power I coveted above all his others.

"Will, I'm so sorry," Alyssa said. She seemed taken aback by my reaction and reached out and touched Will's shoulder, then ran her fingers over his neck, which surprised Casey as much as it did me, because we both looked at each other. In fact, it made Casey clearly and instantly jealous.

"Don't be sorry," he said. "Griffin's right. It was funny."

"You never told *me* that story," Casey said. She took the last drag on the joint, squinting extraferociously as she inhaled. "How did *that* one escape me?"

"Yeah, well, nobody knows everything about anyone." Will, who'd just rolled another bone and was holding it toward me, looked me right in the eye, which made me instantly paranoid. Did he know I was fucking Casey? Following this train of thought was very bad, so I recited the mental mantra I employed whenever I got stoned: *Grass makes you an ass.* It calmed me down, and Will had already shifted his attention to Alyssa. "I mean that," he said to her. "You can develop a whole moral philosophy around that fact. I've been reading Levinas's *Totality and Infinity*. His idea that the Other is an infinite . . ."

Will began explaining Levinas to Alyssa, who was as enthralled with him as he seemed to be with her. I thought he was trying to get into her pants, and while that might solve some logistical problems, I couldn't bear how jealous it was making Casey, so I got up and checked out his room, which never ceased to fascinate me. He had two four-foot-tall speakers pointed out his windows, because whenever he cranked up his stereo he wanted to share his musical taste with the whole quad. A big fan of Black Flag and The Replacements and the Butthole Surfers, he had their posters all over his walls, and though I appreciated these outward signs of allegiance, I found the stuff so impossible to listen to that I wondered if I was lacking in musical knowledge. I needed to add some genre to compliment my personality, to be deeply into *something*. I just hadn't figured out what yet. Will was not only on the cutting edge musically but also technologically: the hutch above his desk was stuffed with green circuitry boards, floppy disks, wire clippers, a soldering iron. He'd programmed his Macintosh to do all sorts of things, like act as an alarm clock and answering machine; he used HyperCard to create outlines for classes and played strategy and role-playing games on it like MineHunter that to me seemed wildly complicated. He was one of the head techs at the college's computer lab and had a campus radio show, "Rumor Will," long musical sets interrupted by programs about the student body and faculty, which he did à la *Saturday Night Live*'s "Weekend Update." He was head of a crew that had the coveted Thursday evening shift at the Rathskeller's downstairs bar. He was so *whole* that you could tell he would make a bright new place for himself in the world. There was a black-and-white poster on his wall of his father sitting in one of those phallic race cars, wearing a helmet and goggles and waving as he crossed the finish line. When I'd asked Will about it, he told me his dad was in a club back home and had built that car from the ground up. And it didn't occur to me that a man who belonged to such a club was rich, or that at my age Will was probably trying to figure out how to get rich enough to belong to such a club.

"You know," Will told Alyssa, "death's right here in this building."

Casey rolled her eyes at me. "Here we go."

"You know what I'm talking about, don't you?"

"No," Alyssa said.

"I'm talking about room nine-E."

"Jesus fucking Christ," Casey said.

"What's in nine-E?" Alyssa asked. She looked at Casey, then at me (and I'd heard all the stories). She was a double major in psychology and biology but lacked a single imaginative bone in her lovely body.

"It's the room where Patricia Wilkes hung herself from the pipes our freshman year," Will explained. "It's been boarded up ever since. Seeing as Miss Alyssa has never been in the presence of death, I say we break in there and have a look."

This was a nice play on Will's part. If Casey was so pissed off at his flirting, for all he cared she could stay the hell put while he took Alyssa on a little adventure. From my end I thought it would give Casey and me some time alone, but she had that look on her face that she got when we had sex: the inwardness of someone testing a physical limit, like a dancer stretching a tender muscle. I'd watch her buck on top of me while this expression came over her and feel like I was almost incidental to her pleasure. All of which is to say I didn't know what she was thinking.

"Why would we want to go there?" Alyssa asked.

"Because supposedly nothing in the room has been disturbed. All of Patricia's family pictures are still inside. Her clothes are still in the drawers. Her Garfield posters are still up on the walls. Everything. It's like a museum."

"Really?"

"You're pissing me off, Will."

I didn't need this from Casey. She had a temper and things could go south between them in a hurry, and if they did there'd be no us, at least not tonight. She'd spend the next few hours, maybe even days, fighting with him, and their fights were notorious. At the beginning of the semester, just before we'd started up, she became convinced Will was having an affair with a friend of hers. The story was that she came into his room and confronted him about it. He was sitting at his computer and turned to her, calmly denied everything, and then went back to the paper he was writing, at which point she grabbed a large flashlight and smashed it right across his skull. Dazed, he stumbled out of his room with his head gushing blood, truly afraid for his life and concussed so severely that his feet were crossing one over the other like he was drunk, while Casey ran after him, sobbing and wailing, "I'm sorry, sweetheart, I'm so sorry, oh, Will, you fucking *asshole,* I'm so sorry." I'd heard this story before I'd said a word to either of them. It preceded them, like the rumble you hear of a train when you put your ear to the rail. Their relationship had this sort of legendary dimension, and I was always impressed by their capacity to conflagrate or implode and inflict harm on each other.

I wanted that. Not the violence, but the intensity of feeling.

That summer, the weekend I'd spent at Alyssa's house, on our last night together, after we tucked Danny in we made a bed of comforters on the floor in front of the television upstairs and screwed during *Austin City Limits*. Afterward, she sat up watching the show while I lay against the couch. Alyssa has large breasts, beautiful and upturned like ice cream curled in a scoop, her areolas brown as cocoa, and I stared at her while she watched the screen, her body's edges traced in light. "I love you," I told her. When she didn't respond, I said it again, and even *she* knew I didn't mean it. But I believed that if I verbalized it the feeling itself might come, as a vine grows toward the nearest higher thing. "I appreciate that," she said, "I really do. But right now I don't feel that way." Then she went back to watching the show.

Alyssa had a boyfriend at the time, Anthony Geddis, who played lacrosse with me. She showed up at all of our games, but I hadn't noticed her until the end of the spring. On break I'd gone to Laguna Beach with a bunch of guys—eight of us piled into a VW bus, road-tripping south to Rosarito—and one afternoon we stood in a circle in the ocean and played a game of tag where the person who was "it" had to spit on someone, and if you managed to dive underwater before the gob hit you, you were safe. While we played we threw out names of girls at school, ranking them in order of beauty and desirability, skankiness and sexual prowess, responding to each like applause-o-meters, supplying inside information when required, and when Alyssa came up the reaction was so thunderously appreciative it could've attracted sharks. At *that* moment I decided she would be mine, no matter what. The minute we returned from spring break I pursued her with a relentlessness even I didn't understand—until she finally broke down that summer. Once we got back to school in the fall, she confessed our affair to Anthony, we started dating again, and by September's end she professed her love to me. "I'm yours," she said, "you win."

Both the victory and the concession repulsed me deeply. A few weeks later, Casey and I started up.

"I think I *would* like to see that room," Alyssa said to Will, without looking to me for approval. I became paranoid again. Was she breaking up with me? Had she been doing it with him all along? Did Will lace my joint with cyanide? *Grass makes you an ass.*

They got up to leave, and since I never took the lead with Casey, I waited to see what she was going to do. She stood up, crossed her arms, and with one hand indicated the door, so I obediently walked ahead. I wasn't sure what to think about this. Maybe she sensed I was kind of reeling, because before we were out of the room she slid up behind me, squeezed my ass and, in what I took to be a boost to my failing morale, sang, "Don't fear the reaper," waiting, I guessed, for me to sing the next line—or at least to buck up.

I wasn't afraid of death so much as getting in trouble. According to dorm rules, the suicide room was off-limits, and Will needed very little encouragement to do something risky. He was currently in an ongoing competition with Johnny Manion, a rugby player and all-around psycho, in which they attempted to do "the craziest thing." The game had started up a few weeks ago and was like a hybrid of Uncle and Chicken. If you couldn't top the other person's feat, you lost, each successive stunt requiring increased levels of recklessness and potential pain. Will began by sneaking into the chancellor's office and replacing the picture of her husband with one of John Holmes, the porn star. Manion considered that bush-league and proceeded to appear in an art-history class completely naked. Not to be outdone, Will jumped from the third story of the chemistry building onto a small sofa. This put him on crutches for two weeks, but sent Manion pondering. A week later, he stood with us outside his terrace apartment during a keg party and, in a moment of inspiration, began to eat moths, plucking them one by one off the wall by his porch light. His lips were covered with moth dust afterward; he looked like he'd been snacking on a crumb cake made of slate. He ate fifteen in all. At this point, Will considered conceding, but then got his nerve back. "I'm still in," he told Manion, nodding determinedly. "I didn't doubt it for a second," Manion said, then vomited in a steady stream at our feet. That was a week ago. Will was planning his next move.

It was a Friday night, but early enough in the evening that in order to break into 9-E we'd need some kind of distraction. There'd be people milling around the halls, playing music, hanging out in their rooms, and since I was a follower in this expedition I let Will sort out the details. We took the elevator upstairs, but Will pushed the eighth floor instead of the ninth. When the door opened he said, "You three go up. I'll be right there." He walked out of the elevator and looked up and down the hall, then said hello to someone. The elevator door closed. It was a slow car, and as we rose we heard the building's fire alarm go off. By the time the door opened on nine, people were heading for the stairs.

We waited in the hallway for the floor to clear out. There was a guy still sitting in his room, blowing a bong hit out the window. "You fucking lemmings!" he screamed over the quad. The three of us were standing in his doorway and he turned around to look at us. "Don't be fooled," he assured us. "It's just another false alarm. It's *always* a false alarm!" he screamed toward the quad again. "So unless I see flames, I'm squatting."

Will appeared at the stairwell and led us to the infamous room. At the end of the hall, 9-E was literally boarded up, with two-by-fours X-ed across the frame. We stood there a minute while Will rubbed his chin. He yanked at one of the boards, even pressed both feet against the wall and pulled, but it was hopeless. They were screwed into the jamb. He looked around, said "Stay here," then opened the window at the end of the hallway and climbed out. Alyssa, Casey, and I watched him step over the fire escape's railing and move out of sight.

A few seconds later we heard a window break. Then the door opened.

"Welcome," Will said, standing behind the Xs in the door frame, "to the suicide room."

He helped us through the spaces between the boards, and closed the door.

I admit my heart was racing. Once my eyes adjusted to the dark—the overhead bulb had long since burned out—I took in our surroundings. The room was noticeably colder than the hallway, and the floor was dusty. Realizing the place was empty of artifacts, I was more afraid for my sinuses than my soul. The bed frame was still here but the mattress was gone. The bureau was empty. We looked up at the pipes but didn't expect to see any signs of a hanging, since we'd all dangled from them in our rooms at one time or other, had chin-up contests or monkey bar races along their length. But Alyssa was impressed that we were actually *here* and, wanting to give Will some sort of credit for his efforts, she crossed her arms and rubbed them with her hands and said, "It's *cold* as death."

Will glanced at me, and we both rolled our eyes.

"How the hell did you get in here?" Casey said.

"The window."

Casey walked over to the broken window and looked down. Alyssa and I joined her.

"I *know* the window, dickweed, but how did you get *to* the window?"

Will pressed between us and poked his head out.

"I climbed over the fire escape," he said, pointing, "then walked along this ledge and kicked in the pane."

The ledge was perhaps two inches wide. It jutted out from the building and was decorated every few feet with remarkable gargoyles. I figured the distance from the fire escape (nine feet), looked for handholds in between (none I could see), considered the height (nine stories), then factored in the nerve and coordination required for such a maneuver—including the logistical difficulty of having enough of a purchase to kick in the window—and I almost didn't believe it.

"You're a sick boy," Casey said.

"You think people really die if they dream of falling and then land?" Will asked.

"That's a myth," Alyssa told him. "Like wanting to sleep with your mother."

"But if it isn't, is that considered suicide?"

"Me," Casey declared, "I'd gas myself. I'd do a Sylvia Plath. It'd be like an eternal whip-it."

"You mean 'the whip-it to eternity,' " I said.

Casey made a face at me. "What-fucking-ever."

"I can't imagine anything more selfish," Alyssa said, "than taking your own life."

I looked down the nine-story drop and considered my own options if I were to commit suicide. Things could go wrong with a hanging. The cord might snap. The pipe might bend and break. Failure could mean brain damage. Same with sticking a gun in your mouth. If you slashed your wrists you might lose your nerve during the time it took to bleed out, leaving you with nothing to show for it but scars that signified your own treacherous neuroses—aces up your sleeves, if you were comparing extreme personal experiences, but ultimately a party trick that embarrassed the magician. Or you could just fail somehow. Fail stupidly. Clumsily. Failure at committing suicide, I thought, could have worse lasting effects on a person than any missed at-the-buzzer jump shot or misspelled word during a spelling bee. It was a real-life failure, a lack of planning and attention to detail that would follow you through your days like a prison record. Fail at *this,* I figured, and chances were good that you'd permanently doubt your ability to carry off anything difficult for the rest of your life.

"I'd jump," I said, but no one seemed to be listening.

The fire alarm stopped. You don't realize how quickly you adjust to noise until it ceases.

"We should probably leave," Will suggested.

We climbed out through the boards, but instead of going back downstairs to Will's room we climbed out the hall window and sat down on the fire escape. Nine stories below, the fire engines had arrived in the quad, their strobes spinning silently, and we sat in the warm night with our feet dangling through the bars and watched as the firemen walked into the building, helmets off, their own keen sense for false alarms confirmed. Hundreds of dorm kids milled around in the red and white light, unaware that all of this was nothing serious, a lie like the one I'd told about my grandfather. And in that quiet moment watching this sight, I enjoyed the nearest thing I can remember now to an animal peace. I was content. I suffered no thoughts of the future, had no stress or worries or responsibilities and was briefly, blissfully aware of this. We were well above the tops of the trees, which were many stories high themselves, and in the building's floodlights they cast massive shadows, the wind playing through their leaves like a long, steady aspiration, as if the world itself were breathing. The fact was I didn't suffer enough from anything to seriously consider suicide or any other self-destructive act, and I wonder now if that's enough to be thankful for. Is a life of such relative luxury and comfort an embarrassment of riches, or a horrible sort of poverty?

This moment was interrupted by the appearance of Johnny Manion, who sat down cross-legged behind Will and pointed at his watch. "Time's running out, Will. The glove's been thrown down, and you've got to make a move."

"I know. I've been mulling it over and I think I'm ready."

"I *know* I'm ready," Manion said. "I'm ready to be *wowed*."

As I mentioned, he was a rugby player, a flanker. He had a beak nose, hooked at the end like a vulture's, bugged-out eyes like Marty Feldman's, and a high head of uncontrollably curly hair. This, I thought, was someone who looked in the mirror every morning and thought: Why? He didn't have the bulk you'd imagine some-one in his sport would need. But I'd played touch football against him, and he was deservedly famous on campus for his speed and split dodge, the latter so devastating it nailed your cleats to the turf. He had thighs that were thickly muscled and disproportion-ately large, like the tires on a redneck's monster pickup.

"It's going to be untoppable," said Will. "It's going to demand your instant concession of victory."

"I'm quaking," Manion said. "I'm listening carefully."

"Honestly, the idea itself is so daring that you might have to concede before I even begin."

"I don't underestimate you, Will, I never have, and what I'm feeling right now, inside my chest, is basically suspense."

"I'm going to kill myself," Will said.

Nobody reacted as if this statement were remotely out of the ordinary.

Manion nodded. "Strong. *Inspired.* Still, I don't believe you."

Casey was ignoring Will, so he leaned toward her.

"I *am* going to kill myself," he said, "because no one gives *a shit* if I do."

He leaned across me to say this to her, and in profile they looked alike, with the same long, delicate nose and Roman profile. He, too, had thin lips and long limbs, and a strong grip that surprised you. He and Casey could be brother and sister.

She rolled her eyes.

"But you're right," Will said to Manion, sitting back. "I'm not going to kill myself. But if I *were* to kill myself"—he leaned toward Casey again—"I'd do it only out of *deep passion*. Because I would've been brave enough to let myself be *shattered*. I would do it as a testament to some sort of *remarkable love,* the kind that you read about in Shakespeare or Tolstoy or who-the-fuck-ever. But something you protect at *all costs.* Do you *get it?*"

Manion cleared his throat. "No. But does that mean I win?"

Will relaxed again and slumped forward, letting his arms dangle through the bars. It was hard to tell if this monologue was simply a performance or a true expression of emotion, but I took it as the latter. I loved being around Casey and Will, because in their presence I felt I was in contact with real feeling. I had the sense, watching them carefully, quietly, that I was witnessing something ineluctable. They needed each other so much they'd already lost the ability to imagine life apart. When you're nineteen years old, need like that is a remarkable thing to observe.

"Instead," Will went on, "I'm going to walk around this whole dorm, along this ledge. And if this ends with my falling to my death, you're going to have to concede, obviously, and you're going to have to tell everyone the version I prefer, which is that I told you I'd kill myself and then went and did it. This guarantees my legendary status at our beloved alma mater. It puts me up there with Patricia Wilkes and that guy who fell off the catwalk at Main last year and Dave Hendrick's three-day acid trip. What do you say?"

"I say you're on."

Will stood up and retied his shoelaces in double knots, then looked at Casey and said, "I'll be back," as if he were an astronaut going out for a pack of cigarettes.

"Whatever." Casey shrugged, though I could tell she was too afraid to look.

"You don't have to do this," Alyssa said. "Really. I don't think it's a good idea." She was too scared to understand the exchange that had just occurred. I found her lack of perception as insufferable as Casey's anxiety for Will, and a sudden feeling of loneliness gusted through me so powerfully I shivered.

"No," he said, "it's not."

He stepped over the fire escape and, with his right hand holding the railing and right foot still on the grate, placed his left foot onto the ledge. He turned away from us, then ran his left palm along the building's face, finding a hold and pinching the brick. He pressed his cheek to the wall and paused for a moment, making some sort of inner adjustment of his body's ballast and a preparatory twist of the ball of his left foot. When he stepped off the fire escape, his whole right side was momentarily suspended over space until he closed onto the wall, his arms outstretched and his legs wide apart, looking as though he'd been splayed against the building by a giant.

He began to move, and it was like watching a starfish advance along the sea floor, his legs and arms active but the rest of his body still, every inch he gained along this horizontal path rippling from left foot to calf to thigh to buttock, from left hand to wrist to arm to shoulder, then expanding out to his right side. Like Will, we forgot about the height out of necessity and were transfixed by his concentration—too focused to be scared. He paused at the window ledge where he'd broken into the room earlier, a stop that appeared to be a physical relief to him, what with its various handholds, easy to negotiate by comparison to moving across the building's face.

He soon resumed, going through the same act of maintaining his balance. After several breathless minutes, he arrived at the building's corner—a stage that required serious consideration—and in a fluid, confident move stepped out of our view.

Alyssa, Casey, Manion, and I looked at one another like we'd just seen someone blip out of existence, then laughed giddily and ran inside.

We began, singly or in pairs, sometimes as a foursome, to follow Will's progress around the building. We went from dorm room to dorm room as he advanced along the perimeter, all of them unlocked and empty since everyone had bolted after the fire alarm, catching glimpses of him as he slid past the windows or waiting two rooms ahead, throwing open the panes and rooting him on. At other moments we just watched silently as he passed, then raced out and barreled into another room. Will moved very slowly, resting for minutes at a time, and certain parts of his journey were dicier than others. At these points we'd separate into pairs, to get a look at where he was stuck or do reconnaissance for any upcoming obstacles—potted plants or empty beer bottles—and call out to one another from our different stations when his position seemed particularly precarious. We were like a bike racer's support team, and as Will rounded the second corner in his Spider-Man crawl he gained confidence and speed.

I was waiting in a room several yards from his position when Casey slid up behind me, pressed her hips into mine, and stuck both her hands in my front pockets. "Find me later," she whispered, kissing the back of my neck.

"Where?"

"I'll sleep in my own room tonight."

"Are you sure?"

"Positive."

She turned me around. She took clumps of my hair in her hands and fed on my mouth, sucking on my top lip, biting it. I grabbed hold of her jeans at the waist and pulled her into me and she climbed up my body, hooking her ankles behind my knees and wrapping her arms around my neck, and we stood there like a circus act. She was surprisingly strong and she seemed keenly satisfied to have climbed me. We kissed once more before she jumped off me, and there was Will at the soot-dark window, either staring at us or—like Casey during sex—focused inward, assessing the state of his body's endurance and balance, working out problems I was neither privy to nor able to understand. He didn't react as if he'd seen us, but he was right there, and the sight of him made my heart jump.

We continued around the rooms as Will approached the home stretch, across the back of the building and around the final corner. "Holy shit," Casey said, in a tone that pained me, "that son of a bitch is going to do it." She and Alyssa barreled out the door to the fire escape. Manion and I were alone for a moment in the last room that Will would pass. We could hear the girls cheering outside. "You can do it, Will," they screamed. "You're almost there."

"I can't top that," Manion said, smiling and shaking his head, his appreciation palpable. "I just can't."

Then he joined the girls on the fire escape.

I watched Will through his last window. The pane was open, so I could've touched him, even given him a little push. Or I could've reached out and held him by the belt, told him the game was over, that Manion had conceded, and helped him climb inside. But games have their own momentum, and I didn't do any of these things before the end, though I want to fast-forward and talk about what became of everyone before I get to that. This is a story about college, after all, and like most people I check the class notes in my alumnae quarterly to see who's doing what, if for no other reason than to compare my life to theirs and get a sense of my place in what feels like a race, even if it isn't one. So:

Alyssa Richardson became a neurosurgeon specializing in hemispherectomy, an astonishing procedure used to treat severely epileptic children. The storming half of the brain is disconnected from its healthy counterpart, or in some cases even removed. These are performed only on the very young, when the organ is most plastic and the remaining hemisphere can take over the tasks of its darkened opposite. It gives patients something resembling a normal life, and I imagine her brother's condition could be said to have inspired this breakthrough. She married her prior boyfriend, and they're the proud parents of Leslie, five, and Danny, three. E-mail her at *geddisbunch@gmail.com* or friend her on Facebook.

Casey Connor went into marketing. She married Manny Swift, MIT '85, who made a fortune in the midnineties developing web-streaming technologies. They had two boys, Will and Toby, and were living quite happily in San Francisco until Casey had an affair with Manny's business partner (I got this part through the grapevine). So it seems she needed to repeat the sort of episode that I had the pleasure of being part of years ago but never got close enough to understand. Casey currently lives in Atlanta; she's a junior VP at Coca-Cola and apparently doing her best to boost their falling stock price. I'm sure she'd love to hear from anyone in the class of '87.

Johnny Manion became a successful commodities trader. He married Alicia Febliss and had four children in quick succession, barely a year apart. He was on the eighty-ninth floor of Two World Trade Center when the first plane hit on September 11. He and three associates immediately decided to evacuate and urged their colleagues to join them, but they were ignored. Some of them had been through the '93 bombing, and they considered this a false alarm. Manion's group took the stairs to their terminus at the sky lobby on the forty-fourth floor, and here they wavered, along with people from offices on other floors who were also uncertain what to do. The mood was upbeat, borderline anarchic, like a high school fire drill. Manion's team decided to return to work, crossed to the other elevator bank, and again Manion hesitated, watching with a sense of dread while the car filled up. He boarded last, just as the doors closed and the second plane hit. The impact ejected his group from the elevator but sent the remaining passengers plummeting to their deaths when the fireball instantly melted the cables. He quit trading immediately afterward and now practices Chinese medicine, something he'd always dreamed of but never had the guts to do.

As for me, I became a writer, and every job I've ever held or choice I've ever made has been ancillary to this task. This means I'm free to embellish, to treat memory as fact or shape it to suit whatever I'm working on. My primary responsibility, I suppose, is to set you dreaming. If that requires me to alter things, then I will, though I can't change what follows because it's true:

Will fell. This was, as he predicted, a legendary tragedy at my college and a defining moment in my life. There he was—a moving, life-sized X—just a few feet away from me, then he stumbled over a gargoyle and disappeared. The fire department turned around and came back to campus, the police questioned all four of us, and Alyssa, Manion, Casey, and I received counseling for the rest of the semester. Will's parents sued the hell out of our beloved alma mater, where nowadays when you open a window onto a fire escape an alarm will sound.

You see, it turns out that Will was wrong about defining moments. We don't invent them; they *happen* to us. And I think about that night all the time. That was the night I woke up. For the first time in my life, I started to feel whole. Because from that night forward, as often as possible, I began asking myself: *What are you doing?* This isn't to say I necessarily do the right thing. It just means that I can't say I didn't think about it. That it can be a beautiful autumn evening, and the best or worst day you've ever known, and it doesn't matter. That given a minuscule ledge or a length of rope, you can contrive your own death, whether you meant to or not.

In the Basement

We were at Nicholas and Maria's house, watching the video of their ultrasound. They'd decided they didn't want to know the sex of the baby before it was born, so the technician had edited the tape for them. But Maria was finishing her residency in internal medicine, so perhaps there were clues in the image only she could see, something about the shape of the fetus's winking heart that indicated a girl, or a rhythm to the dusty blood flow that revealed a boy. If she guessed, she didn't let on. She serenely watched it, as if conducting a conversation with her child, cataloging all the secrets and stories she would tell, the bedside songs she would sing, the mistakes she might prevent. We sat in their living room. It was winter in Nashville and we'd had a week of snow. It was snowing even now. In the mornings I woke to a world of uniform grayness, the trees on the powdered hills bristly and charred, the sky as colorless as the screen in front of us.

I found the ultrasound disturbing. I'd never seen one before and the unborn child seemed to me a mutant creature, barely human. The figure was so striated that it was like looking at the fossil of an embryo, as if the fetus was carved out of bone. It lay at the base of a cone of light, feet up, hands curled near its mouth. When it moved you could see ribs fanning along the axis of its spine, reminding me of the sinuous skeletons of snakes. As the technician moved the probe over Maria's belly, orbiting the child, the image took on a funhouse-mirror quality, the baby's face suddenly elongated like a Munch painting, its eyes two enormous dotted sockets, its head distinguishable as two separate interlocking parts: jaw attached to skull, skull arching over the eyes like a centurion's helmet.

"That's the brain plate," Maria explained. The fetus seemed to stare out at us from the television, then twitched convulsively and came to rest again.

Nicholas said he thought it was a boy. He sat on the couch next to my wife, Carla. He hadn't taken his eyes off the screen, and when he said this he stuck out his hand and gestured, laughing. "It *is*," he insisted, as if it were self-evident, as if proclaiming it made it so. "Look at it," he said. "Look at *him*." And suddenly I saw a clear resemblance to Nicholas in the protruding brow, the discretely prominent chin, the distance from the mouth to the eyes suggesting the same small nose that Nicholas had. And I thought, Of course it's a boy. Of course Nicholas would exercise his will even over Maria's womb. And of course Maria would have a son when she needed a daughter—an ally against Nicholas and this life in which he surrounded and enclosed her.

"Let's turn this off," he said after a while.

"All right," Maria said, picking up the remote to pause the tape. The image of the creature-child hung there, frozen.

We were at that point after dinner when it isn't clear what to do next. Carla got up to get more wine. Maria cleared some plates and followed her to the kitchen, even though Carla had told her to stay put. Nicholas and I had to get up from our seats in order to let them out of the room. He and Maria had long ago outgrown this dank little place, a nondescript brick duplex, but Nicholas hadn't had a job in almost two years. He was eight years into his philosophy doctorate, struggling to complete a dissertation on the pre-Socratics that he'd never been able to explain to me. They couldn't afford to move on Maria's salary alone. To compensate, Nicholas had made all sorts of home improvements. In the living room he'd installed a bike rack hung from the ceiling. For all their books, he'd run track shelving on the adjacent wall. In the kitchen he'd erected a wooden countertop over their washer and dryer, a contraption that folded open on hinges, the machines half visible beneath it like a pair of caged animals. Above their bed he'd wired a pair of reading lights into the walls and built floating shelves into the corners so they could squeeze in the largest mattress possible. Most ingenious was the changing station he'd fashioned in the closet of the nursery, a table that slid out like a keyboard plate with storage for diapers and blankets in the drawers below. Their place reminded me of a nuclear bunker—a testament to Nicholas's insistence on using every inch of space they had. (He'd worked construction to pay for college tuition but now—with a child on the way and an unborn dissertation—he wasn't doing anything.) Despite all this, there was no room in the apartment for a Christmas tree, so they'd hung a wreath over Maria's small piano and stood all their cards below it.

One of them caught my eye, and Nicholas noticed me staring. "She's drop-dead, isn't she?"

It was a photograph of a husband and wife and their two young children, a boy and a girl, the family on a beach somewhere luxurious, though nothing captured your attention like the woman. She was incredibly beautiful.

Nicholas smiled. "Ever seen two uglier kids?"

Their homeliness was as remarkable as their mother's beauty. I looked at the card again. It was a pleasure to be able to stare at the woman so unabashedly. She had long, curly brown hair, blue eyes so pale they seemed lit from within.

The girls returned. When Maria noticed which photograph I was looking at she said "Oh" and tucked her chin into her neck. "That's Lisa."

"Tell them the story about Lisa," Nicholas said.

"You tell them."

"No, you tell it."

Maria sat down gingerly, adjusting her skirt. Then she looked at her chest and brushed herself off, as if she were covered in crumbs. "I don't know where to start," she said.

"Start at the beginning. At school."

Maria reached over to the table, picked up her wineglass, took a sip, and put it down. Marx and Weber, their two German shepherds, squeezed past the coffee table and curled themselves neatly around her feet, having grown noticeably more protective during her pregnancy. She bent forward to pet them, then leaned back in her chair.

"Lisa," she said, "was my best friend in college. We became close when we were sophomores in chemistry, and we shared an apartment together our senior year, the year that Nicholas and I met. She was gorgeous, just like you see her now, but I don't know, she seemed even more so then. Do you agree with that?"

Nicholas shrugged. He ran his palm across his short black hair. When we met them two years ago, he wore it long, down to his shoulders, but now he cut it himself. He was half Russian and a quarter Cherokee, with Asian eyes and the full lips of a Mongol. He'd played football in college, and his body still had some of that absurd mass.

"Go on," he said.

"She was also brilliant. No, that's not even right. She was one of the most intelligent and creative people I've ever met. She was a big star in the English department and a dual major in biology. She could paint, too, and didn't she come to school on a dance scholarship?"

Nicholas nodded.

Maria took another sip of wine. "Anyway, when you were around her you couldn't help but think how nice it must be to have unlimited options in life. And yet you couldn't hate her or be jealous—at least I couldn't—because she was so kind. She was good. She was *good*, wasn't she?" she said to the dogs. They lifted their heads, waited, then put them down and sighed. "She had nothing to be afraid of," Maria said. "I remember that fall we were all talking about what we were going to do with ourselves next, and Lisa had all sorts of glamorous plans—teach English in Japan, work for Doctors Without Borders, go to Africa for the UN. And I supported anything she suggested without question because somehow I needed her to do something spectacular." She looked at Carla. "Does that make sense?"

Carla had lit a cigarette. She'd opened the window by her to spare us the smoke. "Absolutely it makes sense," she said.

Maria paused for a moment. We're close friends, so the silence

133

was comfortable. I poured myself more wine and looked around the room, at all of Nicholas's books, at the bicycle rack and the reading stand he'd made with rollers on its legs and an adjustable desktop so that Maria could work while sitting in their club chair. To make ends meet, she'd been moonlighting regularly at Veterans Hospital, Baptist, and Vanderbilt, seven months pregnant and still picking up killer shifts, twenty-four and sometimes even thirty-six hours on call. And you could look at these things Nicholas had built, these enhancements, as his way of either assisting her or goading her—I wasn't sure which. According to mutual friends, three years ago, before we knew them, Nicholas had an affair with one of his graduate students, and he and Maria separated for a time. One afternoon, after he ran out of fellowship money, he snuck over to her apartment, stole a credit card application from the mail, and applied for it under her name. He used this card to fund his life for the next several months, running Maria into enormous debt. And still, after all this, they reconciled. This was a mystery to me. Why had she forgiven him? Why had he come back? Could people really forget or get over such things? Had he crippled her self-esteem? Or were they willing to go to these lengths simply because they loved each other? "They're either the cursed or the blessed," Carla once said to me, "but I'd have kicked that son of a bitch out long ago"—which at the time I took as a warning. On the other hand, I wasn't sure it was so cut and dried. There's a photograph of the two of them in their living room that I always like to look at whenever I'm over. Nicholas and Maria have their backs to the camera, walking hand in hand along the ridge of some valley in Germany—nothing but mountains beyond and below them for miles. It's fall, so they're wearing sweaters and stocking hats, and because they're on a slope and Nicholas is standing downhill from his wife, they seem the same height, two happy little people, married since forever. And every time I consider this photo, what's clear to me is that it's easier to understand what makes two people let go than what keeps them together.

"Where was I?" Maria said.

"Unlimited options," said Carla.

"Anyway, by the end of that fall I'd already applied to medical schools, and Nicholas was applying to programs in philosophy. But Lisa, I don't know how to describe it. She just shut down. It wasn't exactly a nervous breakdown, but something close. She just withdrew—from me, from school, from everything. All her energy left her. Her enthusiasm. Maybe the weight of her options started to overwhelm her or—"

"Oh, come on," Nicholas said.

"What?"

"You're telling it completely wrong."

Maria hunched slightly, and her eyes went blank.

"Weight of her options?" he said.

Maria wouldn't look at him. "Story police," she said.

"Don't make her such a victim."

Carla and I had never witnessed them quarrel openly, but we'd seen portents, harbingers of fights waiting to happen the minute we left. "*You* tell it," she said, sitting back in her chair. Maria stared into space while Nicholas smiled at the two of us. His teeth were spaced widely apart. I tried to catch Carla's eye but she took a long drag on her cigarette and wouldn't look at me.

"First of all," Nicholas said, "you have to understand that Lisa wasn't some picture-perfect genius. She was a bit of a head case. You'd agree with *that*, wouldn't you?"

Maria didn't appear to be listening.

Nicholas shook his head. "Lisa could be *way* out there," he said. "She had this need for extravagance, so everything she did had to be extraordinary. And if it wasn't she abandoned it—no matter what it was, or who. That fall she was talking about writing a novel, and she even started one at the beginning of the semester. She signed up for a creative-writing class and when she came back after the first session she was so excited she could barely contain herself. She was going to write a novel like no one had ever written before, she told me. She thought it was amazing that a narrative form several hundred years old was still chained to linearity and psychological realism—the same Joycean rant all the smart kids make before they bother to write a word. Then she went to her room, closed the door, and set to work—just like that. I'm pretty sure she was up most of the night. Being manic like that, she'd have made a great surgeon. I was basically living with Maria by that time, so when Lisa left for class the next morning, I went in to have a look at what she'd done because I was dying of curiosity."

"Jealousy," Maria said.

"Please. The pages were on her desk—fifteen, maybe twenty, drafted in one sitting. She wrote this very mannered prose, but it had a kind of energy that immediately hooked you. But it wasn't really a story per se. It began with this long description of an old doorman in the service elevator of an apartment building. He's collecting tenants' trash and going through it, spinning tales in his mind about what he finds while remembering things he's overheard during his rides with these same people. He's got a portable radio with him in the elevator that's tuned to a call-in show, and the narrative shifts from these on-the-air conversations into what's going on in the guest's head. He's a doctor who's explaining the process of separating conjoined twins, giving all this technical material in layspeak, but then it goes into his memories of the actual operation, passages that only someone with Lisa's knowledge could pull off. That's as far as she got, but it was fantastic stuff. It really was. And I wanted to tell her this. But when I stopped by that evening, she was sitting at her desk holding her hair in one fist and striking through line after line with a black marker. She was crossing everything out in utter disgust. So I knocked lightly on her door, and she glared at me wild-eyed and said, 'I'm *working*,' then reached out and slammed it in my face. She dropped the class a week later."

Maria stood up; both dogs, suddenly agitated, rose too. "I need some water," she said, and went to the kitchen. Carla was looking at Nicholas, slightly amazed, as if she'd never seen him before. She was still ignoring me, and I felt a tightness in my gut, something close to fear. Occasionally, a night with Nicholas and Maria could touch off tensions between the two of us. Carla was twenty-eight and had been practicing law for two years. I was thirty-three, teaching the LSAT, bartending, still struggling to wrap up a novel I'd been working on for a long time. When she got frustrated with me, when we really got into it, she'd say I'd been finishing the book ever since we met—an ungenerous, simplistic accusation, I thought, if not entirely inaccurate. What was inarguably true was that there was a growing list of things we couldn't talk about—the hours I'd put in writing that day, if I'd gone for a run, if Nicholas and I went out for coffee. "It must be nice," Carla might say, "to meet for a leisurely chat in the middle of the afternoon." I didn't dare answer. I started editing out all sorts of daily information, minimizing conversations with my family, growing wary of phone calls that tied up our line. "Who were you talking to for so long?" Carla might ask when she got through. *Bitch* was often on the tip of my tongue, and I would've said it many times if her questions weren't apt, her frustrations and fears not justified. Worse, these elisions were changing me: I was a miser with good news, with friends' pregnancies, promotions, new homes. When Carla called me out regarding this pettiness, we sometimes spiraled into vicious argument. In the past few months, we'd said unforgettable things.

Maria came back. "You didn't have to wait," she said.

Nicholas watched her sit, but she wasn't backing down and I thought they might have it out right then. He wanted some acknowledgment from her, even at our expense. He was so unyielding that in a strange way I admired him. He made *no* apologies. He just took. Yet he never talked to me about Maria, as if their relationship was sacrosanct. Once, over drinks, I'd told him about the problems Carla and I were having; bitter, I offered more details than were necessary, all of which he considered thoughtfully. But finally he replied, "Never underestimate a woman's loyalty." I felt so ashamed that I promised myself I'd never discuss my marriage with him again.

"But Maria's right," he said, relenting. "Lisa did shut down for a while, but not because she had unlimited options. She just had no follow-through. Everyone around her was making choices on the fly. Plenty of us had no idea what we were getting into, but Lisa didn't understand commitment. She couldn't accept that making a choice eliminates other choices. She wanted to step up and hit the bull's-eye on the first try. She was so talented, so quick, she had no clue how long it really took to get somewhere."

At this, Maria and Carla simply looked at each other.

"So she overcompensated. We come back from Christmas vacation after Lisa's had her little meltdown, and she's all better. She seems completely restored. We're having dinner together that first night, and out of the blue she announces she's getting married.

"And we're floored. We were like, 'Married? To who? *When?*' And she says she just wants to *get* married, she *has* to get married. We think she's joking. But Lisa's like, 'I've never been so sure of anything in my life. It's what I want. It's what my mother did, and she's happy. I don't want to be one of those women who have to compete in the rat race. I don't want to work insane hours. I want children. I want to be a *homemaker*. Is that such a dishonorable goal?' And then she lists all the qualities she'd come up with for her ideal mate. She really had a list. He had to be financially secure enough to support her comfortably. She wanted him to be handsome, absolutely. She felt strongly that he should have a solid religious background—Catholic, Jewish, it didn't matter, as long as he believed and practiced *something*. It got a lot more specific than that. She'd really put her mind to it. It was all so hyperconscious that I honestly thought she'd gone nuts. And when Maria and I told her she was being obsessive, that this was a misguided grasp at certainty, at a direction, she shot us down. She said we were being hypocritical because we were married already, even though it wasn't official, which was true.

"She went out almost every night that spring, hunting for a

139

husband. It became her job. Her new major. It was the sole purpose of everything she did. She trekked into Seattle and hit the town. She joined a gym off campus. She started going to openings at galleries, to restaurant openings. She asked about the family backgrounds of classmates. She became a database of who was who and who had what. She dragged Maria and me out with her occasionally. And the nights we came along, it was fascinating to watch her size men up, approach them, talk to them or wait until they approached her. And within an hour or sometimes just minutes she'd come back to where we were sitting and compare the guys against her criteria and describe how they'd passed or failed. And the whole time she seemed completely happy.

"But none of them made the cut. I don't think she even slept with anybody. One guy, Thomas, was part of the Heinz or Hellmann's family—directly related to some condiment. Anyway, he took her out regularly and spent many late nights at the apartment, but always left scratching his head. I mean literally. He looked so puzzled that Maria and I started calling him Doubting Thomas during those last few weeks he held on. And suddenly we stopped seeing him altogether.

"By then we were graduating. Maria and I both got into schools in Oregon and Lisa took a job with a think tank in Washington, DC."

"No husband?" Carla asked.

"Not even a boyfriend," Nicholas said.

"Can I see the card?" Carla whispered to Maria, even though I was holding it. Her indirectness made me mildly furious, but I passed it to Maria, who handed it to her, both of us keen to see her reaction to the image—which was one of total indifference.

"Over the next few years," Nicholas said, "we began to drift apart. We were busy. She and Maria didn't speak often. She'd gotten into medical school but dropped out after a year and a half. She took a high-paying job in pharmaceutical sales, then quit. She moved to San Francisco and worked for a dot-com startup and was traveling coast to coast all the time. When she and Maria did manage to talk, Lisa mostly discussed the men in her life. If she was still on her quest, she'd made a real mess of it. She'd had an affair with the married CEO of her company, who was going to leave his wife, then he wasn't, at which point Lisa fell into the arms of some journalist she was involved with back in New York. And I thought she'd arrived at the perfect solution to her own character, because I couldn't imagine her tolerating anyone long enough to get to the point of marriage.

"But maybe a year later she calls to tell us that she's in love. His name's Uzi Levi, an Israeli investment banker. They'd been together for two months, and she goes on and on about how successful and handsome he is, that he's everything she could ever hope for, et cetera. She described this whirlwind romance, how on their first date they flew down to Los Angeles for the evening, had dinner in Santa Monica, then drove to a house he'd rented in Malibu. How when she woke up the next morning the view from the bedroom was of nothing but the Pacific, the dolphins swimming, the whales breaching, all typical Lisa-extravagance. And when we asked her what he was *like* she said, 'All questions will be answered at our wedding.' Again just like Lisa to make such an announcement.

"Have you ever been to a wedding that feels like a horrible mistake? Where every accident seems like an omen? The reception's held outside, and it pours. The bride's father's toast is uncomfortably short. A child wails during the vows. We meet this Uzi Levi and he's thin, balding, charmless—as blunt as a lot of Israelis can be. He had these three girlfriends he'd known since childhood, and they hovered around him the whole time like a bizarre chorus. During the rehearsal dinner, they gave a weird, inappropriate toast, this poem they'd written in couplets full of innuendo about his sexual past with them and his decision to marry outside the fold. And of course it was wrong of us to hold anything against him, because he was the victim of our *own* expectations for Lisa. Everybody's a social Darwinist at a wedding: you want the perfect pairing for a friend. But we just didn't get it. And to see them under the *chuppah* and watch their two families circle up for the *hora*—Lisa's WASP contingent and Levi's clan—it was like some bad comedy of intermarriage, the most insane mismatch. I know it sounds like I'm some closet anti-Semite, but that's not it. They were just so completely different it was hard not to think about them in almost animal terms. Meanwhile, the spectacle of it all was off the charts, and god knows how much it cost. When Lisa and I danced she kept me stiffly at arm's length, and when I asked what her plans were she said, 'Go on my wonderful honeymoon, take care of my wonderful husband.' Everything was so wonderful it was depressing. She smiled, thanked me after the song ended, and then she made her way around the room. Maria and I watched her talk with the other women, putting her hand to their pregnant stomachs and oohing and aahing and showing off her enormous ring—and if this all seems clichéd, it was, and *that's* what stunned us, that she'd transformed herself so utterly. And when she wrote us a thank-you note for our wedding present, she described the private island where they'd honeymooned in excruciating detail: how every couple had an open-air hut and put up a flag when they wanted a meal, how the owner of the resort bred yellow Labs that swam in the surf and ran free in honey-colored packs. I guessed she'd finally gotten what she wanted.

"After that, we heard from her only when we got the birth announcements. And holiday greetings like that card there—pictures of Lisa and her husband and their kids. Until, a few years later, we get another unexpected phone call.

"She'd latched onto the idea of buying a dog for her children, a German shepherd, and as soon as she said this I could envision her mind working through a series of associations back to us. We had two Shepherds and would be the ideal resource to consult about this important decision. She made a little small talk but then went right into it: 'How are your dogs with kids they meet? Are they too protective with you? Did you cage train?' It was painful talking with her. She'd done some Internet research and was full of the concerns that come with superficial knowledge. What about Schutzhund shepherds? Should she buy from a German breeder? It wasn't surprising that she needed a best-in-show dog with impeccable bloodlines. We got a slew of calls from her over the next few weeks—questions about what to look for in terms of temperament, personality, conformity standards, training techniques—but never any sense that she realized we hadn't spoken in years. Did we use treats or vocal praise? Would a male dog recognize a woman as alpha? Did we let our dogs on the furniture? Were they afraid of blacks? Until finally, after this endless back-and-forth, she called to say she'd bought a puppy, as if we were dying to hear what she'd decided. Naturally, it was a bitch Shepherd she'd had shipped from Germany and paid an arm and a leg for, maybe four thousand dollars, and she was going to train it herself. The children *loved* the dog, and she was *so* enjoying their bonding with it and would send us a picture—and that was it. We didn't hear from her again, though a few weeks later we did get the photo, and of course the puppy was gorgeous, and on the back Lisa had written her name: Eva.

"So a few months later, Maria and I had a wedding to go to in San Francisco. We hadn't seen Lisa since she got married, so we called the week before our trip and made arrangements to stay an extra day afterward to visit with her and meet her kids. We were very curious. I remember how giddy we were as we drove up to Pacific Heights. You always have this preconceived idea of luxury that's rarely fulfilled in reality, but not in this case. It was a white house perched on the highest point in the neighborhood, with incredible views of the Golden Gate and the bay. It was sur-rounded by a huge brick wall and had a roof deck like a crow's nest—a widow's walk—with a wrought-iron fence around it. Inside, everything was immaculate and the furniture ultramodern: Viking range, Sub-Zero fridge, shower with jets from five angles, the whole works. After the tour we met the children, who were with the nanny in the third-floor playroom. You could tell the daughter had all of Lisa's intelligence, and the boy was unusually self-possessed, but they were both so *odd*-looking. I don't want this to sound mean but Lisa's perfect features had combined with her husband's in such a twisted way that it made you realize how close beauty can be to its opposite.

"So finally the three of us sit down for coffee. Uzi, Lisa informs us, had been called away on business at the last minute and couldn't join us, which was all we heard about him that afternoon. After we'd been talking for a while, Maria goes, 'Wait, where's the *dog*?' And Lisa says, 'Oh, we don't let her play in the house.' And Maria asks, 'Well, is she out back? I didn't see her.' And Lisa says, 'No. She's downstairs.' And Maria's like, 'What do you mean?' And Lisa says, 'During the day we keep her in the basement.' So Maria looks at me, then at Lisa, and finally says, 'Well, c'mon, let's go see the girl.'

"I'll never forget this until the day I die. Lisa crossed her arms and led us down a narrow wooden staircase to the basement. It was dry and very cool, perfectly clean and bare, as if the house had been vacated or nothing in their lives ever made it to storage. A dim light was shining through the dirty transom windows looking out into the front yard and the flower garden. And in the middle of the room, in the near dark, I could see the kennel—probably the same crate they'd flown her over in.

"A single exposed bulb hung from the ceiling above it, and the moment Lisa flipped the switch I could see the light reflected in the dog's eyes through the bars. It was so small there was barely enough room for her to move. Utterly rigid, she looked at us with her ears pricked up, waiting for Lisa to come to the gate. There was so much love in her eyes, so much patience, as Lisa drew closer, her arms still crossed, and bent down to peer inside. We all stood quietly, and the dog, completely alert, frozen, just waiting, didn't make a sound.

"But *we* waited too. Maria and I were speechless, horrified, waiting like the dog for Lisa to do something, until finally she said, 'There she is.' She gestured toward the animal with her head. 'That's Eva.' She waved at her halfheartedly, her other arm still pressed across her chest. 'Hello, Eva,' she said. This sent a pulse of movement through the cage, which scratched against the floor, jumped slightly. Then Maria looked at Lisa and said, 'Let her out. *Now.*'

"The moment Lisa opened the gate you'd have thought the dog was shot from a gun. She ran out and past us up those creaky stairs. Her back legs were asleep, so she lost her footing and tripped as she dragged herself up, her hindquarters splayed out behind her. And then, at the top of the landing, she *waited* for us in the kitchen.

"The dog was completely out of control. She was so submissive that as soon as I got upstairs and made eye contact with her she pissed all over the floor. She was so desperate for company that she mouthed like a pup, jumping and pawing at us all, barking and running wild in tight circles as if she were chasing her tail, and then she squatted to shit. Meanwhile Lisa was leaning against the door, calmly watching the whole scene as Maria and I tried to settle Eva down. Lisa just stood there, slowly shaking her head. 'You see? This is why we can't let her in the house. She *pees* everywhere. She jumps. She knocks things over. She S-H-I-Ts on the floor. It's just terrible.' And I said to her, 'My God, Lisa, how can you treat an animal like this?' The dog had her mouth on my wrist, pulling at me. And Lisa told me, 'Honestly, Nicholas, I was very patient with her, but it didn't help a bit.'

"Maria and I couldn't stay after that. We looked at each other, and without saying a word we had this silent exchange: Do we take the dog with us? No, we can't. But we will *never* speak with this person again.

"So we left. We made these embarrassed, hurried good-byes, then drove down toward the bay. We didn't say anything for several minutes. I think we were both in shock. And then Maria broke down, sobbing her heart out. You remember how you cried?" Nicholas said.

But she wasn't looking at him, just sitting there, looking at the image on the television screen, swirling her wine.

"Anyway," Nicholas said, "we haven't spoken to Lisa since. She still sends us Christmas cards, though I don't think she gives us a thought. I mean, I'm sure it never occurs to her that we're people she no longer knows. We're just another thing on her list of a million things to do."

It was snowing harder now than before. I could feel the heat escaping through the front door, could see the accumulation rising on the sill and honeycombing the panes, streaming down through the streetlight like so much dust.

"So that's the story," Nicholas said.

Carla and I cleared the rest of the dishes. We told Maria to stay in her chair and rest, and asked Nicholas not to move, though from the living room he said we should just leave the whole mess by the sink; he'd take care of it in the morning. Maria had leaned her head back against her chair, and within minutes she was asleep. We didn't even consider waking her up to say good-bye.

Carla and I walked home. It was beautiful outside, with no cars on the road and no traffic noise at all, and for a long time we just absorbed this quiet world falling around us. The tension I'd felt between us had dissipated in the cold, which forced us to lock arms as we slipped and slid together. Our laughter at each surprising misstep sounded like the only laughter on earth, and we spoke only of the night and the snow until we got close to home. We stopped to look at our house blanketed in powder, as if to make sure we'd taken its true measure. And then Carla said she loved me, that she wanted me to finish my book, that she knew I could. She wanted us to have a child soon. She hated Nicholas, I *had* to know she did, and she didn't want her life to be like Maria's. I assured her that would never happen. I gave her my word, and to make sure she believed me I enumerated all of Nicholas's failures. I rehashed all the unpleasant things he didn't know we knew about him, like I was going down a checklist of faults I didn't have. I talked for a long time, longer than I should have. I kept talking even after my eyes no longer held hers, Carla staring instead at her feet. And in that moment of weakness, I hoped that she might look on me afterward and feel lucky.

When in Rome

Regarding my brother, Kevin, my father would always say, "You have to try to be available to him." I thought he meant that there would inevitably come a time—a very bad time—when Kevin would need my help. Then, my father hoped, I'd have a chance to finally reach him, that he'd take my good advice, whatever it might be, and begin to turn his life around.

I resented this, of course, and thought most of Kevin's problems stemmed from the fact that, for as long as I could remember, he'd always been treated differently than I was, held to a lower standard, and that what my parents needed to do, just once, was to let him suffer some consequences. But our parents died suddenly last year, so lacking any last words on this, or anything else that might constitute their final wishes, I took this urging of my father's to heart and promised myself that, despite failing miserably at it while they were still alive, I'd do my best to honor it in the future.

Any older brother who's telling the truth could list a million such failures, but there's one instance I'll describe in particular.

I'd taken a job in Los Angeles during the summer after my second year of law school, mostly to be close to Kevin, who was managing a restaurant on Rodeo Drive. Kevin started working in restaurants when he was fourteen, busing tables on weekends, then working as a waiter; he'd go in right after school and return home late at night. He never had time for homework, though my parents always managed to act surprised when his dismal report cards arrived. At eighteen, he was managing his first restaurant, and there was good and bad in all of this. He never liked school much—he has ADHD and always resisted taking medication, with predictable results— so his success in this other realm helped his self-esteem. But he also got too great a taste of the wider world when he was too young, exposed to too many rudderless people and too much money, and this killed any interest he might've had in going to college. I'm not saying you can't have a full life working in restaurants, and obviously countless successful people have forgone higher educa- tion. I just thought it was premature for Kevin to be narrowing his choices so dramatically. I always told him he'd regret not going to school, though I couldn't really explain why to him at the time, and in any case he never listened to me. Another thing my father would say about Kevin: he listens only when he's in despair.

As he was that summer. He'd been audited by the IRS in the spring, and it turned out he owed close to twenty-one grand in back taxes—which he didn't have, of course—on top of tens of thousands in credit card debt. So much cash had passed through his hands during the six years of his working life that it didn't make sense he had nothing to show for it. I didn't realize that most of his money had gone to drugs and, at that point, was still going there.

He was living with his best friend from high school, Troy War-
burg, a guy who did him no good. They'd bonded as class clowns
and poor students, both exceedingly popular. An impregnable
force field surrounded their friendship, shutting the family out.
What drove us all crazy was that Kevin didn't seem to realize Troy
actually had a future, which he did his best to squander. At River-
dale Country Day, he was one of the top defensive backs in New
York State, but got busted for burglary his senior year and was
subsequently expelled—a misdemeanor that a lot of top NCAA
programs were willing to overlook. Then during his freshman year
at UCLA, he and some friends stole his roommate's keys, took his
car for a joyride, and totaled it. Furious, the roommate pressed
charges, getting Troy kicked off the football team and stripped of
his scholarship. He transferred to Cal State Fullerton and dropped
out after a semester. Troy's parents were divorced, and his dad, a
bigwig realtor in LA, gave him a job in his company and bought
him an apartment in Los Feliz, near the Griffith Park Observatory.
As soon as he was set up, Troy invited Kevin to live with him, an
opportunity my brother jumped at, much to my parents' dismay.

I had my own reasons for disliking Troy that had nothing to do
with his complicity in Kevin's troubles, starting with his version
of my character, which went something like this: I was selfish to
the point of ruthlessness, perhaps even pathologically so. Everything I did or said was out of self-interest. Nothing I gave was free;
everything I offered was part of some elaborate subterfuge. For
example, when I counseled Kevin to do better in school, what I
was really hoping to do was win my parents' favor as a good son by
forcing my brother to buy into a system where he always ended up

second to me. In fact, my whole sense of self *depended* on oppressing Kevin, along with everyone else. Troy believed it was his duty to remove the foot I'd placed on his best friend's neck. Otherwise, he concluded, Kevin could never be "his own man."

When it came time to argue my case, it didn't help that Troy, at six-four, was a massive, biased referee who was always looking for an opportunity to intervene on Kevin's behalf, preferably physically. I was a state-champion wrestler and not afraid of a fight, but I was a middleweight then, 158 pounds my senior year, and knew my limits. In high school, whenever Kevin and I got into it around him, Troy would wait for my brother to storm off, then bend down to get in my face and recite all manner of mangling threats—"A pop to the bridge of the nose," he'd say, "sends a bone to Caleb's brain." He'd slap my chest with the back of his palm, or press a finger to my forehead, daring me to start something. I never did.

"Call out the bully," Troy liked to say afterward, "and he'll always balk." Thus he'd prove himself to be the brother Kevin would never find in me.

But that night in LA: It was a Friday, and the three of us had gone to dinner at a Cuban place near Venice Beach called Versailles. Troy was mad for their garlic chicken, and he and Kevin got ridiculously stoned beforehand and were so utterly fixated on their food that neither of them could speak during the meal. Troy excused himself right before the bill came, so I paid. I didn't care about the money, but Troy liked to stiff me whenever possible on principle. I'd learned to keep my mouth shut about it, since anything I said would soon be used against me in my brother's court.

We found Troy passed out in the back of his BMW. There was so much smoke inside the car that when we opened the doors it was like someone had set the leather on fire. I told Kevin I'd drive, but he assured me he was fine. "Besides," he added, "I don't want anything happening to Troy's car."

As we drove toward the ocean, I was still in my suit, and exhausted. Leaning back in my seat, I asked Kevin where we were headed.

"Nowhere in particular," he said. "Just driving this fine machine."

At that time, he was wearing his hair long and looked like a skinny version of Vince Neil from Mötley Crüe. He made a cell phone call, perhaps to a girlfriend, and talked cryptically for a while. I paid close attention to the vast, low-slung, palm-tree-lined strip mall that was Venice Beach, trying without success to imagine myself living out here after law school. Troy occasionally piped up from the back, dreaming aloud in his stupor, mumbling incoherencies that sounded like an argument he was having with himself, then passed out again. After he'd been quiet for a time, Kevin relaxed. So long as Troy wasn't a witness, it was all right for us to be brothers.

"What kind of work are you doing now?" he asked.

"Civil litigation, mostly."

He nodded.

"Basically that's when one party sues another," I told him.

"I know that, Caleb."

"I know you do."

"What kind of law will you practice when you're done with school?"

Kevin's younger than me by three years, and when he asks questions like this his voice drops an octave and he stiffens his neck. Knowing so little about the professional world, he mimics the tone of authority—real man-to-man stuff—in order to hide his ignorance.

"I'd love to work in criminal justice," I said. "Defense, probably, where the representation can be so bad. But I've got some big loans. Maybe I can pay those off after a few years of private practice, and then I'll look into it." I liked to take the long view with Kevin whenever possible, to demonstrate that I was thinking about the future. He was so broke and owed so much to the government that I was worried for him.

"Hold that thought," he said suddenly. He pulled over, got out of the car, then stuck his head in the window. "I'll be back," he said, slapping the door.

We'd stopped on a street that ran right down to the beach. I could make out the sand and the whitecaps that burst into visibility before dissipating to black.

"Are we surfing?" Troy mumbled.

I told him to go back to sleep.

Kevin was gone for fifteen minutes. The interior lights flared on when he got back in the car, and I noticed the red irritation around his nostrils and traces of powder. I didn't say anything at first, but after we drove for a few minutes I couldn't help it.

"You're showing," I said.

He looked in the rearview mirror, then wiped the powder off with his finger, considered it, and rubbed the residue over his gums.

"Much better," I said.

"I sense a lecture coming," he said, turning to look at me.

"I wouldn't think of it."

"Because nothing you have to say to me means shit."

"That's fine."

"But I want you to understand that." He was driving fast. "I want you to *know*."

I checked if Troy was asleep—he was—and then leaned toward my brother. "You're sure?"

"Fucking-A yes."

"Well, let me tell you something," I said, holding his eyes as he blew through a traffic light that had gone from yellow to red. By the time he realized what he'd done, cars had already entered the intersection. Kevin did a mad slalom between them, spinning the wheel so hard you could hear his palms slapping the wheel. I was holding my breath—partially to keep from laughing—and clenching the door handle through horns and screeching tires, bracing myself in this Tilt-A-Whirl for the delicious jolt of impact that would crumple Troy's car.

"You fucking *asshole*!" Kevin said after we slammed, untouched, to a stop. "You could've gotten us killed!"

I was bent double laughing.

Then a squad car appeared out of nowhere.

"Oh shit," Kevin said, adjusting the rearview mirror to have a look. "Holy fucking shit."

A small part of me felt delighted, suddenly magnanimous and authoritative. I was about to take over, to calm him down and advise him, when he did something unbelievable. He reached into

155

his jacket pocket and threw something at my chest that burst all over me, then jumped out and started walking toward the police.

It was a plastic bag with at least two grams of cocaine inside. I remember holding my hands up, palms out, away from the gunshot wound of powder on my chest, and thinking—as the cops' headlights and strobes illuminated the car's interior—this was it. This was exactly how everything I'd worked for would get wrecked: by Kevin and his stupidity and his headlong rush to undo something that could never be undone. I sat there waiting for the cop to peer into the open window and end my life.

Even now I could hear Kevin talking to the police.

"My bad, officers," he said. "My brother and I were screaming at each other, and I didn't see the light. Okay, actually, *he* was screaming at *me*, but he does that all the time—which isn't an excuse, so write me up."

I turned to look. Kevin had an arm over his face to shield his eyes from the glare, holding out the other as if to say stop. The cops were yelling at him to freeze. They'd pulled their guns and were approaching cautiously, one of them filling my side mirror, but Kevin kept talking.

"Here's my license and my business card. You guys like steak?"

They told him to shut his mouth and put his hands on his head.

"I manage Tatou on Rodeo. I'll have my chef cook you the best steak frites you've ever had. On me. And that's not a bribe."

"Hands down . . . *now*!"

"Okay, it's a bribe."

He obeyed, pressing his palms to his head; and then, miraculously, the second cop said his name. Off duty, the guy worked security when the restaurant Kevin managed became an after-hours nightclub. There were some guffaws, relieved cursing, and the three of them chatted for a minute or so. I heard Kevin say something that sounded mildly conspiratorial, and they all laughed. The cops told him to be more careful and left.

He cleaned me up when he got back in the car, brushing as much of the coke as he could back into the baggie. My heart was still racing. As soon as he started driving, Kevin went nuts—screaming, hollering, laughing. I didn't react.

"How about that, huh?"

Troy mumbled something.

"Man, you missed it. I put the Jedi *mind*-trick on their ass. Are you up, dude?"

Troy, still half-asleep, told him to shut up.

We came to a stoplight, and Kevin looked me over. There was still a mist of fine white dust on my suit jacket. He smiled and winked once, then squeezed my shoulder warmly.

"You've got to give me some credit," Kevin said. "I saved your ass back there. If I didn't know those guys and they'd seen you covered in that much snow, no legal-eagle career for you, my friend."

I punched him square in the mouth, and would've rammed my fist down his throat if I could. He let go of the steering wheel and cupped his hands over his lips, and I set the parking brake and got out of the car. Then I reached back in to yank him over the passenger seat by the hair—he wasn't wearing a seat belt—and out into the street.

And then I lost my mind. I started hitting and kicking him wherever I could: stomach, ears, ribs, shoulders, face. He flipped over onto his stomach, lacing his hands behind his head to protect himself. He was screaming my name as I dragged him by the hair onto the sidewalk, ripped off my tie, and, with my knee pressing against his spine, laced it around his neck and began choking him. I got quiet and methodical and pulled the two ends as hard as I could until Kevin started gagging. I'll never forget how he tapped my leg, like he was asking for a time-out. But I adjusted my grip and held him taut. He started to fade. It reminded me of when I used to wrestle, when I was pinning someone, and the ref would press his hand under my opponent's shoulders, reaching deeply beneath the two of us with his head turned away, as if he were feeling for something under a sofa; and there'd be that extra beat before he hit the mat—like that one extra beat between hurting someone and ending them—when everything was completely still.

Next thing I knew, Troy was all over me. He'd yanked my jacket over my shoulders and head, and in that darkness I felt the blows in my gut and ribs and face like a train running over me. When the same squad car from before showed up, my shirt was covered in blood, and the officers, again wielding their guns, put Troy on the ground and cuffed all three of us. After they got the story straight, I told them I wasn't going to press charges against Troy, who they'd put in the back of the cruiser—though by then it was too late. They'd found his stash (two ounces of pot, ten grams of mushrooms, a gram of coke) and were taking him in to be booked.

I got a cab home. The last I saw of Kevin that night, one of the officers was tending to the burns around his neck. The shame and remorse washing over me was so intense that I wanted to rush up to my brother and kneel at his feet, to beg his forgiveness and lay prostrate before him until he picked me up with his own hands.

But I did nothing. I said nothing. We just looked at each other once, the moment before I got into the cab.

He was lucky. He cut a deal with the DA, selling out his dealer in exchange for two years' probation. With my parents' support he entered rehab at a facility in Florida, where he stayed for six months and got clean. They had to keep me updated on his progress, because after that night he and I didn't speak for two years.

But the night Kevin called me for help, the moment my father predicted would come, it was with bad news about his financée, Ruth Ann. We'd been speaking with greater frequency in the year since my parents' death, though we didn't see each other as much as I would've liked. I work for Davis Polk, in mergers and acquisitions; they pay me well enough, and in return own the freshest hours of my life and then some. It was close to midnight but I was still at the office and completely buried in a deal. I'd be there till morning.

"Do you have a minute?" he asked.

"Of course," I lied.

He told me that Ruth Ann had left him. He'd come home from work late the night before to find all of her stuff gone—furniture, clothes, even the engagement ring. She'd left a note, and when he tracked her down this morning she admitted that she'd been seeing another man for some time.

"He's some bigwig entertainment lawyer," he said. "She told me that she wants to have a family, get married, and have kids, and that she didn't think I could provide all that." He began to weep.

None of this surprised me. I'd always considered Ruth Ann a killer—as traditional as she was iron-willed—and wished I'd warned Kevin long ago. Despite her big-city veneer and brash, tough-girl chic, she's a Georgia girl—a former model—who's Southern to the core. I could tell she was holding a rip cord—I could practically see it dangling from her fist—that she was ready to pull at any moment in order to land herself with three kids on an estate in Connecticut or a duplex on Park. She was an opportunist, and Kevin would be the guy who preceded all that. She'd tell her daughter about her crazy times working in restaurants and clubs, her oat-sowing days, and the wild boyfriend she lived with ("he had *tattoos*"), talking about all this as if it were her Manifest Destiny to have finally found Daddy. I had dates with women like this constantly. None of them seemed to believe in love; they considered their mothers' hard-won independence a birthright, bitterly enduring it themselves like they were doing hard time. I could see them sizing me up, trying to foresee the give-and-take, the trade-offs, the long-term returns on their investment in me, as if romance were some mutual fund. Partners at my firm married them with the thoughtlessness of Unification Church members, wives who looked over my shoulder at office functions within seconds of conversation. They have the asses of twenty-year-olds and give birth to supremely gifted kids. They spend Fourth of July through Labor Day in the Hamptons and the school year, so far as I can tell from their spouses, convening after yoga or Pilates to air their grievances about their hectic schedules. "That was my wife,"

Trace Motley told me after he snapped his cell phone shut, "and she's very stressed out." It was 7:00 a.m. and we'd been working on a merger for twenty-four hours straight. "Twice a week she's helping organize Dalton's silent auction and it's *just fucking killing her.*" I once had a date with a friend of an old girlfriend of mine; she'd married an exceptionally talented staff writer at a big magazine, whose stuff I read religiously. "She wants another kid," my date said, "but this guy was supposed to write the Great American Novel, and he didn't. So now she's stuck." There's a place in hell for these people.

"I don't know if I can be alone," Kevin said.

"Where are you?"

"At the restaurant."

I knew what was coming, so I closed my eyes to steel myself.

"Can you meet me?"

"Of course," I said.

My eyes were still closed when I hung up. I trudged down to the office of the senior partner I was working with, Charles Hohenwald, and explained that I had a family emergency. "Chucky" berated me for five minutes, reiterating that this was *exactly* why my evaluation was so critical, that I wasn't enough of a team player, until at last he said, "Sure, go ahead. Just be back by two a.m. Keep your cell on, though, and take your BlackBerry too." I thanked him for his understanding, gave him the finger through the wall the moment I stepped into the hall, and took one of the firm's cars to the restaurant.

This place Kevin manages, '57 Chevy, is like the ur-eighties bar, serving up bad nostalgia for the new millennium. A Texan owns it, "an oil guy," Kevin said, and it's sprawling. You walk into a main room the size and shape of a basketball court and every bit as loud, at the center of which is a circular bar. The front ends of four Chevys hang from the ceiling like a metallic teepee, their headlights shining on the patrons below, the just graduated, I like to call them: thick-necked former frat boys out for a fuck or a fight or both. The place serves god-awful Tex-Mex I tried only once, quesadillas stuffed with five cheeses and processed chicken, fajitas made with skirt steak—the shittiest of shitty cuts—that Hispanic waiters bring smoking from the kitchen on iron skillets with all the fanfare of inauthentic cuisine. A mariachi band assaults these morons with songs that always seem to start in medias res. But my favorite is the Shooter Girl, who wears crisscrossing black leather bandoliers over her bare shoulders with shot glasses in place of ammunition, a tequila bottle and lime juice at the ready in her holsters; she's as scantily clad as a stripper, and appreciative drunks stuff dollar bills under the straps. An exposed second level runs along three sides of the main room, and there's a downstairs banquet area for private parties that's as enormous as this one. Both were filled—Tuesday night and the place was jammed—and I couldn't help but wonder if it was always this busy during the week.

"No," Kevin answered when I asked him. "Tonight's some weird exception. The owner, he's just taking a loss. He's got another one down in Austin that loses as much money as you can in Texas. It's a write-off. But that's how he wants it." He leaned closer and whispered, "He practically ordered us to make the cash disappear."

"Meaning what?" I asked.

Kevin looked at me pitifully. "For example, we let the bartenders take their buybacks."

"What's that?"

"Domestic beer here costs five bucks. Customer comes up to the bartender, says, 'Four Buds, please.' Bartender says, 'That'll be twenty bucks.' He rings fifteen dollars on the register, drops a paper clip in the drawer for the five-spot he's just bought back, counts his paper clips at the end of the evening, and now he can afford rent in Manhattan."

"Ah."

"Meaning we close our eyes when the busboys steal a case or two of Pacifico."

"So it's nickel-and-dime stuff."

"Meaning, like, once a week, the head manager hands me an envelope with two grand in it and says, 'Happy Birthday.' "

I shook my head sadly. "Who's fudging the books for you?"

"Nobody."

"Won't it show up?"

"No. We've got this thing we do we call 'the fold.' Maybe once every other Friday or Saturday, about two-thirds through service, we turn off the server downstairs. It's got a glitch we found by accident. It runs maybe an hour behind back-up data, so when we shut it down that time just—poof!—disappears. We pull the register trays at closing, skim the difference, and that's that."

I took a sip of my beer. "Don't do that, Kevin."

"You mean don't look a gift horse in the mouth? Fuck that. Plus if I say no, what am I, a squealer? They'd fire me in a second."

"It's still not good."

"That's the least of my worries right now."

He did look like hell, his eyes red and puffy from crying off and on, and he had two days' growth of beard. We'd already been talking about Ruth Ann for a while, and to get his mind off her, I'd changed the subject. He was wearing a double-breasted, eggplant-colored suit that hadn't been pressed, that he must've worn the night before, that reeked of the grease-haze that had hung on him his whole life, but especially here.

"You know the thing about Ruth Ann?" he said.

"No."

"Well, her feelings always come in twos. She'll tell you she's happy about something, over and over again. Totally supportive. When I got this job that's all she said: 'I'm so *happy*, Kevin, it's such an *opportunity* for you.' But at the same time she felt something else. It always came out sooner or later and erased *everything* else that came before. After a couple glasses of wine she'd be like, 'You're better than that place. I thought that the minute I walked in there. I took one look and thought: What's Kevin *doing* here?' And I'd go, 'That's not what you said.' And she'd say, 'Are you surprised?' So, fuck me. 'Of course I'm surprised.' And then she'd be like, 'This is why I don't tell you anything.' "

Kevin *was* better than this place, I agreed. I would've liked to see him running an establishment that was far more upscale, with fine service, a different clientele, and real cuisine. A restaurant that taught him that better things were possible. Where he didn't close an eye to buybacks or skim money. He'd had that at the Mesa Grill but got fired for talking to customers about investing in his own venture. A place like '57 Chevy must make you hopeless, and that's something I didn't want him to be.

"Forget her," I said. "Think about it. What if you were mar-

ried? What if you'd had kids and she'd done a one-eighty on you
then?"

He shrugged.

I don't think he'd heard a single word. "Can I tell you something about her? Something you don't know."

He looked at me.

"Do you remember when you guys were moving a few months
ago, and you stayed at my apartment? You know what she told me?"

"What?"

"She said she was going to raise your family in Georgia. She
had it all mapped out. You'd manage the country club where her
father's a board member. She ever tell you that?"

"No."

What more could I say? For instance, about what I really
thought of her? That same night, after he left to go to work, Ruth
Ann and I drank and talked for a long time. I finally set up the fold-
out couch in front of a high window that faced Jersey City—that
fallen-over-Christmas-tree view—and she was dressed for bed,
her gown as sheer as a cobweb. When I said good night, she put her
arms around me. "Why can't Kevin be ambitious like you?" she
asked. "If Kevin had all this"—she indicated the river and park in
between, as if I owned the whole of Gotham—"we'd be happy."
Then she kissed me, full on the mouth. Ruth Ann's no lightweight
beauty, and it took everything I had to walk to my room, close my
door, and, after what seemed like a lifetime, gently press the lock.
At breakfast the next morning I looked for signs of discomfort, for
a shred of guilt, but we had coffee together like nothing had ever
happened. She even invited me to run with her in the park. Of
course I'd never tell Kevin about this, since it could only doom me.

Then my phone rang, the office number showing on the screen. I stepped away and pressed my ear to the receiver, stopping my other ear with my palm.

It was Kelly Winslow, an attorney I was working with on the merger. "Everything all right?" she asked.

"Getting there," I told her.

"Good. You know how Chucky said to be back by two?"

"Of course."

"*Don't* be late," she said.

"Gotcha."

"You're America's Most Wanted, Caleb."

When I came back, Kevin asked, "Work?"

I nodded.

He looked at his watch.

"You guys must be billing like mad."

"I'm not billing right now."

Kevin smiled broadly. "Come on," he said. "I don't believe that."

"Hey, I'm here, not there. I ain't billing."

"Come on. I'll bet if you, like, took a break from a case to, you know, take a nice long shit, followed by a round of golf, the client pays."

"Negative."

"You're killing me."

"Maybe other people. Maybe at other firms. Not me."

"Because you're so upstanding?"

"Because them's the rules."

"Look me in the eye and tell me you've never once fudged."

I looked him in the eye. "Never."

"Come on," he said.

Of course I had. But if I were even the slightest bit corrupt, everything about me was corrupt. When it came to Kevin's assessment of my character, there were no nuances. I'd be Troy's version again; I refused to concede my advantage.

"The stakes are too high," I insisted.

Kevin clucked his tongue. "Look," he said, "give me a hand with something."

He got up and led me across the crowded floor. As we went toward the kitchen, a black busboy in a skull-and-crossbones do-rag crashed into me with a tub of dirty dishes. "Watch where you're going, white boy," he said, and continued plowing through the crowd. We entered the kitchen through swinging double doors. There were five cooks still working the line.

Kevin said, "*Hola*, Enrique!"

"*Hola*, boss!"

"*Es mi hermano,*" he said, pointing at me.

"*Hermano!*" the cooks repeated, then did the same thing that every worker in every kitchen my brother has ever managed has always done the moment I turned my back: they all laughed.

He led me down some slippery metal stairs, as narrow and steep as a fire escape ladder, then through a winding hallway lit by the occasional single bulb. It was like a mine shaft. Here we ran into another black guy, dressed in a suit, his jacket big as a cape, and sporting a flattop; he must have been close to seven feet tall. Kevin introduced him as Traylor.

"Are you bringing down the register trays?" Kevin asked.

"Five minutes."

"I'll be waiting."

We kept walking.

"Lurch back there?" he whispered a second later. "Top power forward at Georgia Tech. Gonna go, like, first round his sophomore year. Two games into the NCAA tournament he pulls down a routine rebound, lands funky, and blows out both ACLs. Now he's an assistant manager in the food service industry."

"Sad."

"Yeah, but here's the fucked-up thing." Kevin double-checked that he was out of earshot. "He can't read."

"Seriously?"

"He's completely illiterate. He can add and subtract and do numbers, but words? Forget it."

Kevin's office was like every shitty manager's office he'd ever worked in, with nudie Budweiser posters on the wall, the depressing grid of server schedules, purveyor numbers, a litter box for the mouser, except in this one there was a gaping hole in the Sheetrock in the far corner the size of a door. And on a large card table were some twenty rows of neat piles of bills: ones, fives, tens, twenties, fifties, and hundreds.

"What happened to the wall?"

"Oh." He grabbed an adding machine from his desk and placed it on the table, removed the rubber band from the first pile, counted it lightning fast by hand, then punched in the amount on the calculator, the ticker making a sound like a sprinkler as the number printed on the register tape. Then he rebanded the wad and dropped it into a brown paper bag. "We got broken into three weeks ago. Fucking morons tried to blow up our drop safe. See this?" He went over to a black metal box the size of a cat carrier that was bolted to the floor with a circle of soot traced around it. He kicked it with his boot, and it gonged like he'd hit the side of an aircraft carrier. "It's where we put our money every night. You could tape five sticks of dynamite to this thing and it wouldn't budge. Which our friends the robbers must have figured out, since they didn't make a dent in it."

"It's good that it held."

"Not really. They managed to fuse the safe's door. And they vaporized the cat."

We looked at each other and immediately fell into hysteria about the cat. I don't know why we found this so funny but we were laughing so hard we were breathless. Wave after wave kept pounding us until Kevin came up for air—I'd just recovered myself— and said, "Puss-in-*Boom*," and that paralyzed us all over again.

"Phew," he said finally.

I wiped my eyes and asked, "So what do you do with the money?"

He shrugged. "I take it home. Make the deposit the next morning."

I envisioned him going to his apartment in the middle of the night, Ruth Ann asleep, and sitting down in his smelly suit on the couch, maybe pouring himself some vodka, and dumping all that dirty cash on the coffee table. And it *was* dirty cash. Singles and fives and twenties that had been crumpled in pockets, used as coasters for beers, stuffed under registers, rolled up and stuck into nostrils, folded into stripper's garters. Then I thought of Ruth Ann waking up in the morning and looking at that pile while Kevin slept. Because he'd *want* her to see it, just to show her that he was around a lot of money. But she'd think it wasn't all that much, then pour a cup of coffee and continue to plot her escape.

Traylor came into the office just as Kevin finished the count. He was carrying two register trays in his arms. My brother, it occurred to me, was always surrounded by enormous men.

"What'd you get?" he asked.

"I got"—Kevin looked at the tape—"$56,782."

Traylor looked at his own tape. "Ditto."

"Take the money home tonight, would you?"

"Can't."

"Why not?"

"Driving to Poughkeepsie with my wife after we close."

Kevin glanced at me in a moment of telepathy. "What the fuck's in Poughkeepsie?"

"Mother-in-law."

"What about Dana?"

"She left an hour ago," Traylor said.

Kevin sighed. He was about to pull rank. "All right," he said. "Do the trays."

We sat silently as Traylor added up the money from the two other registers, cross-checking his totals against the bartender's, and while he clicked away at the calculator I watched the back of his close-cropped head, his shoulders the width of a bear's, and I confess that I imagined putting a book in front of his face and a gun to his head and making him tell me what it said on the page.

"Walk me out," Kevin said to me when he finished, then picked up the grocery bag and we left.

We walked down Seventh Avenue for a while, talking about

Mom and Dad, nothing remarkable or profound. It was a pleasant fall night. I checked my watch again. It was just after 1:30, and I thought that the political thing to do would be to return to the office now. But then I thought, Fuck it. I'll be back at two sharp, no sooner or later. They get enough out of me. That, and I didn't want to interrupt this moment. Because this seemed about the best Kevin and I could hope for: just passing time together, with a temporary reprieve from the past. Just talk and walk the street as brothers, no big deal. And then emotion got the better of me—that desire I've had all my life for his forgiveness. It wasn't that I thought I could've been a better brother. It was that I realized there'd been periods in my life when I hadn't given him a thought. He *was* all I had. I'd been hatching schemes for us, things I thought of very early in the morning when I got home, all the places we could go, and I wanted to tell him.

"You got time for a quick drink?" he said.

"Absolutely."

"There's a place my friend manages nearby."

We walked downtown two blocks, then turned west on 16th.

"I really appreciate you coming by tonight."

"It's no problem."

"I think I'm solid enough now that I won't blow my brains out if I'm alone."

"Never blow your brains out over a woman. Let alone Ruth Ann."

"Seriously, though. I appreciate it. I know you're busy."

"You'd do the same." I wasn't sure of that but I wanted to believe it.

"I would," he said.

I took his shoulder and stopped him. "You mean that?"

"Yes."

"Then I have a favor to ask."

He looked at my hand, then back at me. I could tell I'd suddenly made him nervous, that I'd somehow imposed on his sad time.

"Go on."

"I want us to start from scratch," I said. "Erase all grudges. I see brothers all the time and I wonder why *we* can't be like that. So why can't we? Let's start *now*. I pick you up, you pick me up. You cover me, I cover you. We're friends. We make a *commitment* to becoming friends, from here on out. Everything else, all that's past, and we just forget about it. We chalk it up to being young. I know I can do it," I said. "But I want you to do it with me."

Kevin stared at his shoes while I talked. He even shook his head once. And when he squinted at me, you'd have thought he suspected some kind of trick, that I'd scammed him or was trying to embarrass him. It was an expression that was totally at odds with what he said next.

"Nothing would make me happier."

He stuck his hand out, and we shook. Then I pulled him close and held him. "Let's get that drink."

That's when the guy hit me. I felt the crack behind my ear and it sent me sprawling into a parked car. I blacked out for a second and came to on all fours, watching blood from my head drip *one two three* between my fingers onto the pavement. I heard my brother say, "Whoa! *Whoa!*" Dizzily, I rolled over onto my back and leaned against the car door.

A black kid was pointing a revolver at Kevin, who had both his

172

hands up in the air. The kid wore a bandanna over his nose and mouth and a black hat pulled down over his brow, and between these his eyes were livid.

"Don't," I said.

He now pointed the gun at me; I could see the torpedo-glint of the bullet tips in the cylinder. They looked like snakes peering out of a pit.

"Empty your pockets," he said.

Still woozy, I reached for the wrong jacket pocket. While I was feeling around in it, he cracked me across the bridge of my nose with the grip. Blood immediately poured from my nostrils into my palms, warm and copious.

"Hurry up!" he said.

"He's *giving* it to you," Kevin said.

The kid pulled the hammer back and put the gun to Kevin's forehead, pressing him back with the barrel until he was sprawled on the hood of the car. "Shut the fuck up."

"Here," I said. I'd found my wallet and held it out toward him. It shook in my hand.

"The watch," he said.

It was a Rolex my father had given me for my college graduation.

Kevin sat up, offering his own wallet. "Just take our money."

The kid pistol-whipped him across the cheek, opening a gash, and Kevin covered his face with his arms.

"Please!" I said, holding out the watch. He took it.

"Mother*fucker*," Kevin said.

The guy put the gun to Kevin's head again. "What'd you say?"

"Nothing."

"Get on your knees."

Kevin lowered his arms away from his face. Blood was dribbling down his chin and onto his shirt. "I'm sorry."

"I said get on your *fuckin' knees*."

Kevin slowly sank to his knees, then dropped his hands at his sides, staring straight ahead like a zombie. A strange silence fell over us, a beat that seemed deliberative, because the kid looked at Kevin as if he'd posed a question, and then, having arrived at the answer, put the gun to my brother's temple and said, "Close your eyes, bitch"—to Kevin or to me, I wasn't sure. But Kevin obeyed. "Caleb," he whispered.

I screamed.

The kid sucker-punched him. The blow sent the grocery bag flying from Kevin's grip, some of the stacks of bills tumbling out. Stunned by its contents, he squatted down over the bag like it was an animal he had to cajole toward him. Then he stuffed the few stacks back into it and bolted down the street, laughing hideously.

It took the cops several minutes to get to us, and by then the guy was long gone. In the meantime, Kevin and I tended to each other's wounds. The gash across his face was bad—maybe three inches long—and needed stitches. His lip was split wide open, and two of his teeth were loose.

I got off comparatively easy. The back of my head had already stopped bleeding. My nose was fat and broken—re-broken, I should say. I'd busted it wrestling in high school. It had a hump in the middle and also curved slightly to the left. Now, I thought to myself, I can get it fixed.

The whole process with the police—from going to the station to filing the report—took nearly two hours, and at one point I excused myself to call the office, prepared for another dose of pain from Chucky, but he was surprisingly understanding. I'd lucked into a rare lode of sympathy. "Wife and I got mugged two years ago behind Lincoln Center," he said. "Guy beat the piss out of me too." Then I remembered seeing him come into the office with the same black-and-blue raccoon's mask around his eyes and sinuses that I'd have tomorrow, and I recalled I'd reveled in the story of his beating.

"This is officially the worst twenty-four hours of my life," Kevin said.

"Let's get you to a hospital," I said. The police were finally done with us.

"I'm so fucked."

"Come on," I said. "You need your face and mouth looked at."

"I want to go home."

"Kevin . . ."

"I don't have insurance, all right?" He shook his head and stared at the sky. "Look, I'm sorry you lost your watch and some credit cards, but I just lost fifty grand that wasn't mine." He was on the verge of tears. "I fucking want to *go home.*"

"All right," I said.

We caught a cab and headed uptown and sat quietly for most of the ride. My nose felt like a balloon slowly filling with water. I leaned my head back and watched the streetlights whip by. Kevin started laughing, and when he smiled his split lower lip opened like a V and exposed the black clots of blood around his teeth.

"What's so funny?"

"I've never seen you so scared in my life. Oh," he said, "that was almost worth fifty thousand. You had that wallet out and it was shaking like a leaf."

I started to laugh too.

Then Kevin's laughter turned into weeping. "What am I going to do?"

"I'll take care of it. Don't worry about the money."

"What does that mean?"

"That I'll represent you. Cover you. Whatever."

"You'd do that?"

"Of course."

I was about to tell him my plan: I wanted him to open a restaurant somewhere upstate. Somewhere quiet. I wanted out of law. I wanted us to be a family.

Then Kevin's phone rang. He looked at the screen. "Well, well," he said, flashing the caller ID. "It's Ruthie."

I listened as Kevin told her the story of our mugging, without any embellishments or embarrassing details. Would that come later? I wondered, him elaborating on how scared I'd been? I didn't care. I could still see the cylinder and the bullets.

"My phone's dying," Kevin told her. "Ruthie, no, I don't think you should . . ." But then the phone went dead, and he sighed.

"She wants to come take care of me."

"So let her."

"I don't know."

I sat up straight as the world fell forward past my head, then righted itself. I felt something slip in my nostrils, and the blood poured out again in a rush.

"Jesus," Kevin said. "Should I have this guy take you to a hospital?"

"They're just going to pack my nose until a specialist can see me."

"All right."

"Not all right," the cabbie protested. "Very not all right! You messing up the seat!"

"Let me come up to your apartment and get a towel or something," I said.

"Sure. I can get Ruth Ann to stop at the Koreans'. What do you need?"

"Lots of gauze."

"Give me your phone."

He called Ruth Ann while I bunched the front of my shirt to my face. I rested my head against the seat and let the blood run down my throat; it was thick as honey and filled my belly until I felt sick.

Ruth Ann met us at the door in a T-shirt and jeans. For 4:00 a.m., she looked perfectly awake.

"Look at you two," she said. "Y'all have just been beat *up*."

I took out my BlackBerry and phone and sat down on the couch, making an effort not to look while Ruth Ann fawned over him and kissed him, something I could never bring myself to watch.

When Kevin went to the bathroom, she slid next to me. "Let me have a look at you, Caleb. Can I touch your face?"

I'd stopped bleeding. "No," I said, "it hurts too much. Just give me the gauze and I'll get out of your hair."

She brought me the gauze and watched while I plugged my nostrils. "Did he tell you?" she asked.

"Yes."

She was staring at my face. "It's not a final thing."

"What does that mean?"

"I love your brother."

"I do too."

"But I have to *manage* him," she whispered. "I have to *mother* him. He gets . . . stuck. I don't want to do that my whole life."

"Then don't," I said. My eyes were swelling shut. "Just don't drag it out."

Kevin had emerged from the bathroom. His shirt was off and his face was clean, but his lip was still bleeding. "Maybe I do need to go to the hospital," he said, then brightened. "Caleb's going to help me," he said to Ruth Ann.

"Help with what, sweet?"

"Legal representation. I mean, if I need it."

Ruth Ann blinked twice, and looked at him so blankly, I could see her filing away this new fuckup or piece of bad luck for her closing arguments. She had a mug of hot tea in her hands toward which she shifted her attention, sipping it carefully.

"Well, bless his heart," she said.

I got up. "I'm going home."

"Here," Ruth Ann said, "I'll walk you out."

She held the front door open, flipped the switch on the strike plate so that the latch bolt wouldn't lock automatically, took my arm, and led me to the elevator. I pressed the button, and we watched the car rise floor by floor.

"I've been confused," she said.

"That's okay."

"You don't hate me? You'd be able to forgive me if Kevin and I worked things out?"

"Of course."

"Why don't you let us take you to the hospital?"

"I'll be fine."

"All right," she said as the elevator arrived.

I just looked at her.

"I'm going to kiss you," she said. "I'll do it gently." She kissed my cheek and I let her smell envelope me, that alchemy of shampoo, perfume, and the earthy sweetness of her makeup. Strangely, Ruth Ann was the closest thing I had to a woman in my life. I stepped into the car and turned around, and she waved as the doors started to close. "You're a good man."

My father's older brother, Saul, died of colon cancer when he was fifty-two. I met him twice in my life, and both encounters were unmemorable. Divorced, he lived in California near where his three grown children had settled, and we never visited his family there. Like his father, he was afflicted with poor health. He was overweight and suffered early-onset Type II diabetes; he had a heart murmur and, in his late forties, developed chronic stomach pain, which he put off seeing doctors about because he feared them, so he died of a treatable disease. In my view, Saul's fragility and mismanagement of his body explained my father's daily exercise regimen, a half-hour set of calisthenics that we called his Jack LaLanne routine, and his dietary rules: one glass of wine at dinner, and no deli food whatsoever. "Pickled meats," he'd say, "smothered with pickled cabbage, plus a pickle on the side, all of it washed down with a cream soda. As much salt in that meal as there is in the sea."

There's a reason I bring up Saul here. My father always said he wanted Kevin and me to be close, which seemed somewhat hypocritical because neither he nor Saul ever made any effort at all; and my father, like Kevin, always portrayed himself as downtrodden. Saul was four years older, and although I didn't know him much better than I did their parents, who died before I was born, my father's stories about his brother's abuse were legion. When my father was eight years old, for example, and had just learned to roller-skate, Uncle Saul took him to the Steuben Street hill, a giant descent in Middle Village—they grew up in Queens—where the big kids raced everything from soapbox derby cars to sleds. They also set up a slalom of soda bottles, which skaters bombed down forward and backward, weaving their legs through magically, and my father, who wanted to try a run, had asked his brother to hold his arm while he got the feel for the turns. But after a few yards Saul let him go. He kept his balance long enough to reach lethal velocity, then crashed into a parked car's fender and knocked out his two front teeth. And once, playing tag at their house, when my father tapped him "it" through one of the windows opening onto their patio, my uncle slammed the pane shut and broke his hand. On a trip to Ocean City, Maryland, Saul convinced my father to sunbathe with him on their hotel's roof deck. He lathered him in baby oil and offered him a reflector for his face, which my father obediently tucked under his chin; he said he'd be back with lunch in a few minutes but didn't return for an hour—a desertion that put my father in the hospital yet again, this time with second-degree burns. I admittedly took a sick joy in these stories. Such casual abuse came easily to me when Kevin and I were younger. To this day he bitterly recalls the time I convinced him to rescue a bee drowning in my cousin's pool, and, to my delight, it stung him the moment he plucked it from the water. But these stories also helped me make some sense of their characters: both had total recall of every transgression they'd suffered at their brothers' hands, and their memories, it seemed to me, were their worst enemies. "I've a grand memory for forgetting," says Robert Louis Stevenson. What happiness in that statement! When we were boys, Kevin's carefully nurtured sense of injustice drove my dad crazy, which conferred on me this bit of wisdom: we are quickest to object to things in others that we don't wish to recognize in ourselves.

My favorite Uncle Saul story occurred in Miami. My father was thirteen at the time, already fitter and taller and stronger than his brother, growing in both stature and confidence. One day they went swimming together and, after idiotically racing fifty yards out, got caught in a vicious undertow. Boys are always nearly killing themselves like this, and of course there were no lifeguards present, so my panicked grandparents, seeing their children sucked down the beach and, for all they knew, out to sea, ran to the hotel to get help. The current drove my dad and uncle into a coral reef, which they climbed in exhausted desperation, cutting themselves badly. They were safe, though, and should've waited there for help, but since they couldn't see their parents they panicked. Saul convinced my father that he could leap far enough off the reef to clear the current, or at least would have enough strength to swim through it, a remarkably stupid idea that my father accepted at face value. He was almost immediately slammed back against the coral, slashing his arms and legs to ribbons, only to pull himself up and, at his brother's urging, try it again. His fourth attempt was interrupted by the hotel's pool lifeguards, who'd paddled out in a rowboat. It was back to the hospital for my father, and the next year Saul went off to college, for all intents and purposes exiting his brother's life.

Which brings me to my uncle's death. After Saul learned he was terminal, he invited my father to spend a week with him in London. In his forties, he'd befriended a very wealthy cousin of ours named Lee who'd made a fortune in the car-wash business. They both liked food and women, serial philandering having blown up their marriages, and in many respects they were brothers who'd chosen each other. They spent the last decade of my uncle's life carousing together and since by then Saul had only a month to live, this London trip was clearly the last fling, and Lee rented them a townhouse. My father and uncle hadn't spent this much time under the same roof since their teens, and I had always been curious about this trip. During the two years that Kevin and I weren't speaking, I asked my father about it, because I wanted to believe this might shed some light on my failed relationship with Kevin.

When I asked what he remembered about that week, my father thought about it for a long time and finally said, "Not much."

"No talks you had? What sort of stuff you did?"

He considered this and then brightened.

"Well," he said, "one night we went to these boxing matches at this private club Lee belonged to. It was a black-tie thing where they served dinner beforehand. They'd set up tables around the ring, so close that when the boxers hit each other you'd occasionally get sprinkled with sweat and blood. The room wasn't that big, but it was oak-paneled and stuffy, and the acoustics were amazing. When a guy got hit you could actually hear the air getting knocked out of him, and just by that sound you realized how strong they were, how fast and powerful. It was the most beautiful and violent spectacle I've ever seen. And at the end, no matter how brutally they'd beaten the shit out of each other, they hugged at the final bell."

Recalling this, he smiled, but he hadn't answered my question. They'd arrived together at the end, after all, and I wanted to know what they'd said, if anything, whether there was a reconciliation, a last grasp at closeness, or if they'd even tried. He didn't say, though, and I could tell he didn't want to talk about it anymore, and this now makes me think of Kevin. Because these distances between siblings, I suspect, might be a birthright that's as strong and arbitrary and ineluctable as love; yet because we feel we must honor this accident of our relatedness, we try to swim against it again and again.

After I left Kevin's apartment that night, even before the elevator reached the lobby, I realized I'd forgotten my BlackBerry and cell phone on the arm of the couch. I went back upstairs and checked the door to make sure Ruth Ann had locked it. She hadn't, and I stepped inside ready to reprimand them of how very dangerous this world had just proven itself to be.

And there they were: Kevin, Ruth Ann, and the kid who'd mugged us—the busboy from the restaurant with the do-rag. They were standing around the kitchen table with the money piled on it like a sandcastle.

I walked up the stairs, stared at the three of them for a second, then collected my stuff off the couch. "Can I have my watch back?" I asked.

The kid looked at it, then took it off his wrist and tossed it to me.

"He wasn't supposed to take that," Kevin said.

Ruth Ann had fixed her eyes on the floor.

"We needed a credible witness," Kevin explained.

"I get it."

We stood there for a time. With the gun stuffed under his belt, the busboy stared me down. I was still afraid of him.

"How do you know I'm not going to turn you all in?"

Kevin shrugged, then smiled until his lip split open again. "Because we're starting from scratch."

I turned around and let myself out, careful to set the latch bolt; then I closed the door and checked it to make sure it was locked.

It was breezy outside. Kevin lived near the East River, and when the wind blew the air tasted so thickly mineral that it was like you'd just put a penny in your mouth. I figured I'd hurry home, clean myself up, repack my nostrils, drink some coffee, watch the sun rise, and head in to the office. There is no early where I work, no "first one in." We're round the clock. But I would impress Chuck with my diligence, we'd bond over my wounds, and I'd work my way back into his graces.

Meanwhile, I'd leave the suit and shirt hanging on the door for the cleaners. I wished I could see their faces when they inspected this job, and that almost made me want to drop it off myself: the suit and shirt lying on the counter, the fabric starched with coagulation. For a while they'd wonder what the hell had happened. They'd pick up the pants at the waist, the jacket at the shoulders, shaking their heads at how they'd been set up to fail. It would be impossible to remove all the blood.

Middleman

In the fall of 1980, my parents enrolled me in seventh grade at the Trinity School—a tony, Episcopal private school in Manhattan that was all boys until ninth grade. So my two best new friends, Abe Herman and Kyle Duckworth, were thirteen-year-olds on the cusp of, among other things, coeducation.

Beanpole thin, with a chest so concave a dog could lap water from its indentation, Abe Herman had the gift of imparting debilitating self-consciousness upon anyone within ear- or eyeshot. We sat directly across from each other in English (discussion-based classes at Trinity were taught in the round), and I often marveled at how Abe could unseat the confidence of even the most assured students simply by shaking his head and piteously staring at them while they spoke; or, if he was really in the mood for disruption, shielding his eyes with his hand, as if stupidity that intense could somehow blind him, and looking in the opposite direction. You might think this was motivated by envy, that Abe was shy or inarticulate and his scorn was a preemptive strike against those who would scorn him, but that wasn't the case. Abe was brilliant. Annoyed by his behavior and frustrated by his ability to silence anyone in class, our teacher, Ms. Cheek, would pounce on him in response, assuming an advantage in the element of surprise: "Well, then, Mr. Herman, what do *you* think Marc Antony is telling his countrymen here?" And Abe, leaning back in his chair with his arms crossed, would smile broadly to show off a mouth fat with braces. "I think that Antony is using irony to stab Brutus and Cassius the way they stabbed Caesar. I think he's using his sharp tongue to rip their honor to *shreds.*" He would stare at Ms. Cheek, who, defeated like the rest of us, could only shake her head in unintentional mimicry.

But he was thin, as I said, and small—doomed, by cosmic justice, to a post–high school growth spurt, denied height when he needed it most—so outside the ordered confines of class he was often singled out for beatings by larger kids who were sick of his lip. You wouldn't be surprised to see Abe getting slammed into a locker between periods, ineffectually pounding on the back of whoever had tackled him, delivering rabbit punches and liver shots so weak you'd think he was throwing the fight from the start. We met when I lifted Sammy Munson and Ad Schacht off him, then knocked their heads together and kicked both in their respective asses with a karate one-two. (After seven years of public school, I knew a thing or two about winning a fight.) "It's about fucking time," Abe mumbled from the floor. He looked down at his shirt, buttoned his sprung buttons, then tamped his high head of thick, brown hair. "Well, help me up," he said, sticking out a hand. After I pulled him upright, he gave his lapels a tug and slapped my shoulder. "Come to my bar mitzvah next weekend," he said, and hurried to class.

I'd been to a number of bar mitzvahs earlier that year—bar

mitzvah *receptions*, I should say. These parties were held in places like Leonard's of Great Neck or the Tudor House, with entire floors dedicated to video games like Missile Command and Sea Wolf, all with unlimited credits, so the kids would leave the parents alone to drink for as long as possible. But Abe's was the first bar mitzvah *ceremony* I'd ever been to, and I was awed. The raised *bimah,* with the drawn curtains of the Holy Ark behind it, reminded me of a stage. I had to wear a yarmulke, and I dug the costumes of the synagogue—the square tefillin like a little top hat, the tallith a varsity scarf. I was impressed by Abe's fluency as he sang up there, the force and clarity with which he chanted the haftarah, how deep his voice sounded as he read the prayers—not that I knew the names of these rites or understood much of what I was seeing at the time. I understood only that because Abe had gone through this ceremony, he wasn't just the center of attention, he was now a man. It was held in the morning, and afterward, all of us—Abe's whole family and Kyle, the only other guest Abe's age besides me—went to lunch at Adam's Rib. I kept a loose tally of the gifts he received, the checks big and small, and, vaguely jealous of the whole affair, at dinner that night I asked my father, who was Jewish, why I had not been bar mitzvahed. Did that mean I wasn't a man?

"No." He wouldn't look at me. He was focused on his baked chicken. He liked to eat the bones, which he was in the process of destroying. "You're a man whether or not you're bar mitzvahed. You're a man," he said, "because you've turned thirteen."

So was I a Jew?

"Strictly speaking," my mother jumped in, "no."

"Why?"

"Because *I'm* not. And it comes from the mother."

"What are you, then?"

"I was raised Methodist, but I don't believe in organized religion. Or God, for that matter."

I let that conversation quietly sail by.

"Can *I* be a Jew?" I asked, thinking it was like joining a sports team or deciding on an activity at camp. My mother sat forward, folded her arms across her chest, and leaned her elbows on the table. She stared at my father and shook her head sadly, as if to say, I told you this was coming. And my father, who could look off conflict with the best pro quarterback, said, "We'll talk about it"—like that would put an end to this.

We ate in silence for a long time. You have to picture our dining room. First of all, it wasn't actually a dining room. It was an area just off the kitchen—a sort of gigantic nook. There was a long row of windows to our right. We lived on the Upper West Side, and the view from our third-floor apartment was primarily of the giant blue-brick Con Ed power station across 66th Street. To make the space seem bigger, my parents had installed a mirror that covered the facing wall, which had the side effect of making me horribly vain. I looked at myself *constantly.* I was looking at myself now— my brother was sleeping over at a friend's house, so I had an unobstructed view—and at my parents' profiles. I had my father's curly hair, though it was brown, not black, and his unevenly aligned eyes, the right set slightly lower than the left like some Cubist deformity. I also had a big head. I don't mean in terms of ego, just outsized, blockish, like The Thing's or John Travolta's. (You were a forceps baby, my mother was fond of saying, as if to regularly remind me that tools were required to pull me from her vagina.) And yet my

father and I were both in denial about our proportions. We looked
terrible in baseball hats but often broke down and wore them. From
my mother, I received her bright blue eyes and, because I could
spend hours drawing, *zitzfleisch,* according to my father. Yiddish,
he translated, for "sitting meat," but clearly not for my curiosity,
since I didn't ask him to teach me any other words. All of this is to
say that I knew myself as partly them, physically and temperamen-
tally. But there had to be more.

"Is my name Jewish?"

"Jacob is," my mother replied, "yes."

"What about Rose?"

"That's a stage name," said my father. He had literally cleaned
his plate.

"What's our real name?"

"That is your real name."

"What was it before?"

He shrugged his shoulders like he could barely remember.
"Rosenberg."

"I like that," I said.

"Do you?"

"It's distinguished."

"You think?"

"Maybe I'll change mine back."

For reasons unknown to me, my mother found this hysterical.
So I did what I normally did when I didn't get a joke and laughed
along with her. As for my father, well, he excused himself from the
table by saying, "I have to make a call."

Of course, asking to be Jewish didn't mean I *wanted* to be Jewish. That particular night, I just had Jews on the brain. Beyond what I'd seen that morning, I didn't know a thing about them. And when I told Kyle I wanted to become one, he talked me out of it.

"You don't want to be a Jew," he said. "If you became a Jew you'd be a convert."

"What's wrong with being a convert?"

"Converts are boring. They only talk about one thing."

"What do they talk about?"

"Being converts, idiot."

"Check."

"Plus everyone wants to kill them."

"Converts?"

"Jews."

"Like who?"

"Like Germans, for one. Palestinians. And I'm pretty sure Egyptians."

It suddenly made sense to me why my father changed his name.

"Would you really want to be someone everybody else wants to kill?" Kyle asked.

I shook my head.

"Good," he said. "Then it's settled."

Which brings me to Kyle. Close friends called him Kyle, upperclassmen called him Duckworth, but on all athletic fields he was known as Duck. The name was a mark of respect for his speed, like calling a 150-pound Rottweiler Baby. He was one of the city's top cross-country runners in his age group, a must-pick in the touch football games we played on Trinity's rooftop AstroTurf, and had a starting slot waiting for him on the high school lacrosse team his freshman year. He was blond and slit-eyed, with high cheekbones and a pronounced jaw, a puka-necklace wearer who, after returning from his Christmas vacations in Barbados, was accused by Abe of bleaching his hair. "It's the sun and saltwater," he protested, though his mop was as white as Billy Idol's. "I swear." He was also a daring clotheshorse who affected a preppy style at school that flirted with multiple dress-code violations: loafers with no socks (questionable) and corduroys that bordered on jeans; Lacoste shirt (illegal) with the collar turned up, over a turtleneck (legal) and under a seersucker suit or blazer—the various color combinations of which he wore year-round.

As for myself, I was "full of potential," according to my teachers, but didn't have the mind that Abe had; athletic as well, but no champion like Kyle. I was shorter than the latter, taller than the former. My claim to some distinction was that I was an actor, like my father, who made a living doing voice-overs. I'd done commercials and radio dramas—*Mystery Theater, The Eternal Light*—and I'd had parts in a couple of motion pictures and Afterschool Specials. Just that fall, I'd starred in a Saturday morning series on one of the networks that was canceled almost as soon as it aired—thirteen and out, as they say. My career wasn't born of some driving, Jodie Foster–like talent. I just fell into the business. Through a friend of my dad's, I'd gotten a nonspeaking part in a made-for-TV movie that became a speaking one by the end of the shoot, and that started the ball rolling. Admittedly, I had no real gift besides precociousness and the ability to listen and follow directions—which is all your average child actor needs. Perhaps the fact that show business was, in a manner of speaking, a family business made the whole thing seem relatively banal to me (*We can't live on love alone at City Center*, I heard my father say every morning on NPR) and made almost no impression on Abe or Kyle. Still, because I had spent so much time among adults, with grown-up responsibilities and a salary to boot, there were skills I possessed in excess, namely a willingness to perform when necessary and the fearlessness that required. And if there was a quality I had in spades, it was confidence—without correlative achievement, maybe, but confidence nonetheless.

And I had a keen sense, even at the age of thirteen, for the attributes I lacked, so I was drawn to Abe and Kyle for their respective gifts, as they were to me for mine. We became, I like to think, amalgamations: we hoped to steal some of one another's best, each one the fulcrum to the other two, a threesome in balance, with no individual's select powers giving him alpha-ascendancy over the rest.

But there was something else Kyle had that Abe and I didn't, and that I confess I coveted, and for which I would have been willing, without hesitation, to forfeit our friendship at the drop of a hat.

He had a beautiful older sister.

Like her famous *Born Free* counterpart, Elsa Duckworth had a touch of the leonine in her appearance. She was regal in bearing and had a thick head of blond hair that she could poof up into a face-framing mane. At first glance, she and Kyle closely resembled each other, with the same WASPy contours, the strong jaw and ice-blue eyes; but upon closer inspection, and I inspected as closely as secret inspection allowed, she had a fuller face, almost pudgy in the cheeks, with very small, thin lips—an old woman's lips—and large, round eyes that always seemed wide open. "She looks," Abe liked to say, "like a stick's just been stuck up her ass." Because of her diminutive mouth, lost in that feline face no matter how much lipstick she applied, her eyes were the best place to gauge her reaction to anything or anyone, which in my case was the same dull, sleepy indifference you see on big cats lazing at the edge of the prey-filled, Serengeti Plain.

Kyle, on the other hand, could get a reaction out of his sister almost effortlessly, with an ability I envied bitterly and an approach I instinctively rejected, which was to piss her off. She was a senior at Spence that year and had a curfew of 1:00 a.m., so on the Saturday mornings after I slept over she'd wake up groggy and irritable to the sounds of us playing Atari in the TV room just off the Duckworths' kitchen. Walking past us on a trip to the fridge in her blue flannel nightshirt, she locked into combat with Kyle almost instantly.

"Do you have to make so much goddamn *noise?*"

"Fuck you, Elsa," Kyle said. "Go back to sleep."

"I'm *parched,*" she said. "Is there any orange juice?"

"How the hell should I know?"

Watching Elsa open the refrigerator door, I saw her wide eyes widen further.

"You drank all the goddamn orange juice!" Elsa turned her back to us while she opened the top cupboard, her calves flexing as she got on tiptoe to check her hiding place. "And where are my graham crackers? Did you eat my graham crackers, you little shit?"

"Jacob ate some too."

"Who?"

I raised my hand.

"I bought those for *me.*"

"*You* didn't buy them. *Mom* did."

"But I put them on the *list.*"

"But you didn't pay with your own *money.*"

"Whatever. I had proprietary rights."

"Don't hit me with your SAT words, you fucking cheater."

Yes, it was quite the scandal. There was a rumor that Elsa had hidden a pocket dictionary in her panties when she took the SATs and consulted it during a bathroom break—an accusation that could jeopardize her hopes of acceptance to Princeton in the fall. (She wanted nothing more than to attend Princeton, where her boyfriend, Toby, was a freshman.) I didn't know any more details about the alleged cheating, nor, I think, did Kyle, but any mention of it put Elsa on her heels with fury, as it did now, and she stormed out of the kitchen without food or drink.

But I stole a peek at her, or anything having to do with her, every chance I got. The Duckworths' East Side apartment was laid out like a giant L, with the kitchen and TV room at the bottom end, and the dining room, bedrooms, and living room perpendicular to the long hallway that comprised the column on top. Going to Kyle's room, I often stopped to gaze in the open door of Elsa's bedroom if she wasn't around, at her queen-size bed (fit for a queen) with its radiant peach sheets, at her bulletin board ruffled with swimming and riding ribbons, and, most of all, at the collage of pictures she'd assembled on her far wall.

Collages were big back then, and the few girls I knew at that age combined photographs of models from fashion magazines, cutouts of odd catchphrases (Do it up!), product names, movie stars, lines from jingles (Ooo, la, la, Sassoon!), and logos (the Neptune trident of Club Med, for instance, or pictures of faraway camps they'd attended, like Antigua Adventure or Outward Bound). They glued these onto thin rectangles of cardboard, the items overlapping, the Elmer's glue warping and buckling them into oddly curved shapes like a 3-D topographical map.

But Elsa's collage was different. It was gigantic, filling the whole peg-boarded wall of her bedroom, as big as the mirror in my parents' dining room but reflecting her desires instead of her image, the elements secured not with glue but with white thumbtacks. There were spaces between the photographs, between the Spence and Princeton pennants, between the snapshots of her other lovely girlfriends set tastefully apart, as if each party picture were itself a perfect memory to be cherished, the *only* party like it, these images and icons organized, so far as I could tell, into four discrete quadrants of parties, places, boys, and goals, each demarcated by the exposed gray pegboard beneath—the X/Y axis of Elsa's identity. There were no models or movie stars on that wall, though there was one picture that I couldn't help but dream about, shot down-beach, of Elsa in Barbados, sitting cross-legged on a jetty in a bikini, her head thrown back while the bay's waves lapped the pilings below, her bleached-blond hair hanging down to touch the top of her inverted heart-shaped ass—her own *Sports Illustrated* swimsuit spread. There was a quote running the length of her wall, right below the crown molding, that she'd written out in red marker: GO CONFIDENTLY IN THE DIRECTION OF YOUR DREAMS! LIVE THE LIFE YOU'VE IMAGINED! And at the wall's center, at the intersection of the axes, was a picture of her boyfriend that I can conjure even now: Toby has long, curly brown hair that he's slicked back off his forehead, manelike as Elsa's; he's tan, his cheeks reddened by sun and reflected river light after a day of rowing crew; he's wearing a denim shirt with the top four buttons undone to reveal a hairless chest; he's standing in a circle of friends, laughing so hard that he's bent from the waist as they spray him with champagne. Elsa is visible in the background, her small mouth open as wide as possible with laughter, her hands and elbows pressed together in a WASP-girl clap.

"What the hell are you doing?" Kyle said.

"Nothing," I said, hurrying from Elsa's doorway to his room.

Most of what I knew about Elsa was from these brief glimpses. East Side life at the Duckworths' was like that: mysterious, private, and, most of all, *roomy*. Kyle had his own room, Elsa hers, as did their younger sister, Kirsti, who was barely pubescent and thus invisible to me. There were three bathrooms and a living room that, so far as I could tell by the pristine condition of the furniture, was never used. It was different from life at my West Side apartment, where I shared a bedroom with my brother that abutted my parents' bedroom, which abutted the living/dining area that in turn abutted the narrow kitchen. I did my homework in a large walk-in closet off the front hall. In the morning my father would walk around wrapped in a towel and at night (or whenever I had friends over, it seemed) in nothing more than briefs, his Fruit of the Looms bulging with what looked like a huge stem of grapes. If the Duckworths' apartment was in the shape of an L, ours was an O, and we all filled it like the Tootsie Roll center of a Tootsie Pop. Not that I perceived myself as deprived, mind you. Nor did I associate Mr. Duckworth's blue-suited, Wall Street, seven-to-seven workaday life with greater worldly success than my father's I-don't-know-on-Monday-where-I'll-get-paid-on-Friday freelancer's life. No, it was simply that in the Duckworths' world, indifference to one another—even physical avoidance, if necessary—was a spatial possibility, a luxury that was both taken for granted and respected. People in this universe had lives that could remain separate—a fact so remarkable to me that I decided it deserved my full attention. Consequently, I slept over at Kyle's house every chance I got.

And perhaps because I hung around so often, the day eventually came when I stepped into Elsa's line of sight.

It was taco night at the Duckworths' house. Forget what you've heard about high-powered career people in New York never spending time with their kids. Without fail, every Friday evening Mr. Duckworth cooked homemade beef tacos, and every time I could finagle it, I was there to eat them. He would mold the tortillas into shape by sautéing them in oil and folding them in half, then he stuffed them himself with chili he'd made from scratch and baked them to crisp perfection. Next he chopped up all the fixings (onions, green chiles, lettuce, tomatoes), grated the cheese and put out the salsa, which he freshened with cilantro that he grew in a box on his windowsill. It was an involved process, so much so that Mr. Duckworth didn't have time to change out of his work clothes in order to have things ready at a reasonable hour. He just draped his suit coat and tie on a chair, put on his favorite apron—*Inside Trader*, it read—and got to work.

I liked Mr. Duckworth. He sported a military haircut, looked like a tough-guy version of David Byrne, and always seemed to be squinting like Clint Eastwood, mostly when Kyle spoke. True, Elsa had inherited her small, pursed mouth from him, but on Mr. Duckworth it conferred a look of autocratic determination. Plus he *reeked*—a big word, back then—of authenticity. He'd played college lacrosse for Johns Hopkins. He was very strong and regularly challenged Kyle and me to arm wrestle him at the same time. "I'll use just two fingers," he'd say, then pound the backs of our hands into the kitchen table. Plus he knew stuff he quizzed Kyle about during dinner, manly-man trivia we'd need later on. "If you're shaving," he asked, "do you rinse your razor with hot or cold water?"

Kyle shrugged. "I don't know. Hot?"

"Wrong! Cold won't dull the blade!"

And he stuck up for me. The first night I slept over at Kyle's house, I called my parents for permission. They wanted to know the address, which I had to ask Kyle for. "You fucking idiot," he said. "You don't know my address?"

"Hey, Kyle," Mr. Duckworth said, "what's Jacob's address?"

"I don't know."

"You fucking idiot!" he shouted, and then genteelly gave me the number.

He was big into physical labor (you couldn't get my dad near a shovel, let alone a tennis or soccer ball), and one Saturday morning early that fall he drove me and Kyle out to the three-acre lot he'd bought near Georgica Pond in East Hampton. All of us wore flannel shirts and jeans, and we spent the whole day chopping, piling, and burning weeds, briars, and brush. Toward the end of the afternoon, he took a small charcoal grill from the trunk of his Jaguar and cooked what seemed like the best burgers I'd ever eaten. On the drive back he did the only inauthentic thing I ever saw him do. We'd crossed the 59th Street Bridge and were headed up Third. Kyle, who could sleep anywhere, was passed out up front, while I sat in the middle of the white-leather backseat. Mr. Duckworth liked to drive very fast, and when a cab came to a sudden stop ahead of us, he checked his rearview mirror and my expression at the same time, then said, "Hold on!" as if it were life or death, and swerved around the obstacle without slowing his pace.

"Wow," I said. "That was close."

Mr. Duckworth nodded seriously. "Fucking idiot," he said.

Of course, I knew a performance when one was delivered, and performers like to impress. That Mr. Duckworth cared made me like him even more.

"Thanks for taking us today, Mr. Duckworth."

"Thank *you*. You worked very hard."

"I like working hard," I said.

Kyle, his head thrown side to side during our near miss, was snoring.

Mr. Duckworth looked at me in the mirror again. "Jacob, I want you to remember something. And I know you will if I tell you. It's very important. It might not make sense now, but it will someday."

I waited.

"Getting inside is *everything*," he said. "When you're outside, you might not think you're good enough. Don't believe it. Just get in there first. Then you'll figure it out."

He was staring at me in the mirror again, and I nodded

seriously—he was right, it didn't make sense—and I said what my father always did when he was given directions. "I'm with you."

As for Mrs. Duckworth, well, she was another matter entirely. The kids got their blond hair from her Norwegian genes, and their blue eyes too. She always wore pearls and was what my father called "an attractive woman." Like Mr. D, she worked on Wall Street and possessed the same Brooks Brothers seriousness. But I was convinced she didn't like me. I'd heard her talking to her husband in the hall one evening, complaining that I used too many towels. She always seemed oddly out of it, which could be unnerving. She caught everything mid-sentence, then bobbled or dropped the ball. Kirsti loved to tell endless, meandering stories at dinner, chock-full of exhaustive detail and labyrinthine digressions, these narratives ending on a punch line only she found funny. An instance of Mrs. Duckworth's attention proceeded as follows:

Kirsti: "And then Laurel and I went to the nurse's office to get a Band-Aid and—"

Mrs. D (shifting her attention from the underside of her plate, which she has lifted in the air to examine): "Nurse? When? Were you sick?"

Mr. D: "Edna, listen to the story!"

Kyle: "Yeah, Ma, c'mon!"

Mr. D (to Kyle): "Don't talk to your mother like that!"

Kirsti: "She broke the Bunsen burner and cut her finger."

Mrs. D (taking Kirsti's hands and examining them): "Which finger? Is it infected?"

Elsa (rolling her eyes): "Mork calling Orson."

Kirsti: "It was *Laurel's.*"

Mrs. D (waving both hands in the air): "I don't understand why you two were cutting class."

And when it came to watching sports, she was terrible. She couldn't get the terms right, calling a field goal a touchdown, a home run a goal. True, she knew when to celebrate. The Duckworths' TV room was just off the kitchen, and we'd all jump up together. But the whole family (not including me) would scream, "It's called a *safety*, Mom." To which she took a sip of her drink and, still smiling and giddy with cheering, said, "Shush."

One Friday evening, Kyle and I were sitting on the couch watching the Yankees on Channel 11. Kirsti, the little overachiever, was doing her prealgebra homework at our feet. Mrs. Duckworth was making another round of margaritas. Elsa was talking on the phone to a friend, standing by the stove and indifferently following the game, the cord stretched so taut it had lost its curls. "*Tell* me," I overheard her say. "I love a good schadenfreude."

Then my father's voice came out of the television.

Give, he intoned, *to the United Negro College Fund. Because a mind is a terrible thing to waste.*

"That's my dad," I said to Kyle. To anyone. To the air.

"That black guy?" Kirsti asked.

"No, the voice."

"Bullshit," Kyle said.

"Don't use that language!" Mr. Duckworth said. "And let your friend talk!"

"It is," I said. "That's him."

Elsa pressed the receiver against her chest. "That's your dad's voice?"

It was, I explained, it sure was. Watch TV with me sometime, anytime, and you'd hear my dad everywhere.

"Call you back," Elsa said to her friend.

Dinner conversation that evening centered on me. Even though I'd spent enough nights at the Duckworths' that I could get up from the table and raid the refrigerator like any of the children, Mr. and Mrs. D had no idea what my parents did for a living or, for that matter, even where they lived. In fact, the sum total of their knowledge of my family was written on a note taped above their secretary's desk since the first night I'd slept over: Rose, 787-3858.

Given that most of their friends were probably bankers and lawyers, it must have piqued the Duckworths' curiosity as to how a person actually made a living doing commercial voice-overs, let alone paid their child's tuition at the Trinity School, and Elsa in particular peppered me with questions. First I explained how a voice-over was recorded, with the actor sitting in a soundstage or studio, sometimes with a screen running the commercial behind him; I described the craft required to narrate a twenty-eight or sixty-second spot, allowing for the copy's rhythm and speed; I elaborated on the difference between a regional and national commercial, between residual and nonunion pay, even what the letters in SAG and AFTRA stood for.

"This is boring," Kyle said.

"Oh, really?" Mr. Duckworth said. "Can you explain to Jacob what I do?"

Kyle crossed his arms. "Not exactly."

"Then shut your trap," said Mr. Duckworth. "Sorry, Jacob. Please continue."

In closing, I ran off as many of my father's commercials as I could remember, all the brand names and brought-to-you-bys he'd tagged with his bass baritone. *York Peppermint Patty*, I said. *Get the Sensation. From Peter Paul.*

"No way!" Elsa cried.

Because steak without A-1 is a mis-steak.

"Shut up!"

I couldn't stop. It was a miracle: My everywhere-heard-but-nowhere-seen father had made me visible to Elsa. *Timex. It takes a licking and keeps on ticking.*

"I hear your dad *all* the time," she said.

"Me too!" said Kirsti.

"Who's this?" asked Mrs. Duckworth.

Kyle just shook his head.

But I kept going, moving from my father's achievements to my own acting career, and quickly narrated my whole résumé on TV, in movies, and on radio.

"I had to listen to *The Battle of the Warsaw Ghetto* for history class!" Elsa said. "And that was you?"

It was. I mentioned the national commercial I'd shot for Frosted Mini-Wheats, and how the residuals I'd made on my one line— "But the kid in me likes the frosted side!"—had helped my parents pay for private school.

Mr. and Mrs. Duckworth looked at each other.

Elsa turned to her brother. "How come you never told me about this, Kyle?"

"Why the hell would I tell you anything?"

"Very funny boy," Mrs. Duckworth said, spilling some of her

drink on her blouse and then shifting all of her attention to dabbing her sweater.

"Jacob," Elsa said, "that is *really* impressive."

I'd never thought so until that very moment.

"And *how* much," she asked, "did you say you could make doing this?"

That night after dinner, Elsa did something I'd never seen her do before: she showed up in Kyle's room. He and I were shirtless, switching off doing curls in front of his bathroom's full-length mirror and listening to *Emotional Rescue* when she appeared at his door.

"Do you think you could get *me* in commercials?" she said.

I was resting from my set while Kyle knocked out his reps, and though he wasn't very demonstrative, I detected a slight shiver of disgust at her question. I don't think for a moment that he suspected I desired his sister. I actually doubt he conceived of her as being an object of any affection whatsoever. What bothered him was her invasion of his privacy.

"Sure," I said, "call me at home Monday night." And for the second time in weeks, my father spoke through me again. "We'll talk about it."

Love lives in the future, and by the time Elsa called me that Monday, we'd already taken many long walks together along Georgica Pond (in my fantasies we always seemed to be wearing sweaters), swam together with dolphins in Barbados, and danced away the night at Studio 54, since that nightclub's name was tacked on the parties' quadrant of her wall. Love is also a planner, so I'd arranged an appointment for her on Thursday afternoon with my agent, Donovan Chambers.

"Excellent," she said once I told her. "What should I wear?"

I'd leave that up to her, but at Donovan's request I recommended that she learn a monologue from a dramatic work of her choosing, in case he wanted her to read for him. Elsa could make an entrance, no doubt, but performing was another matter entirely. I had no idea if she had any talent or not, and she expressed as much trepidation about this part of the process as I felt. I told her that I'd be happy to see her beforehand—hinted, even, that it would be a good idea—and coach her, if she was interested, which she was. We agreed to meet at 4:30 on Central Park South, by Columbus Circle. She'd take the bus there after school so we could go over her monologue a few times, then walk to my agent's office together.

That Thursday was unseasonably cold. It was late October, very clear, sunny, and windy. Before leaving school, I was seized by a need to present myself to her in some sort of official capacity, so I changed into my soccer uniform, complete with cleats, shin guards, and the little Trinity Tiger paw on the chest of my overlarge sweatshirt, which I wore hood up, looking like a miniature monk. I rode the 104 bus down Broadway and got off in front of the GW Building, the tower funneling the wind mercilessly around the Coliseum and Columbus Circle. Ridiculously early and buffeted by gusts and self-doubt, I retreated into the 59th Street subway entrance and passed the time looking at the comics on the racks of a Bengali's kiosk, warmed by the metallic blasts rising up from the tunnels. But I was coldly certain that Elsa would discern, as if with X-ray glasses, my black little heart slamming in my chest and, just like her dad with Kyle, would call me out.

But she didn't. She was all business, arriving promptly at 4:30. By then I was waiting for her on the corner of Central Park South, nervous to the point of nausea. The crosstown bus she was on kneeled with a hiss and vomited a group of passengers, the last of whom was Elsa. She was dressed for school and her hair was pulled back in a ponytail, but she was wearing more makeup than I'd ever seen on her and, like Kyle, had given some personal touches to her outfit. She had on saddle oxfords with white ankle socks and her Spence uniform's blue, green, and yellow cardigan skirt. On top, she wore a white Ralph Lauren button-down, the happy Polo player riding over the small mound of her breast; underneath that, a green Lacoste shirt, collar up; and underneath this, a white turtleneck with blue stripes that looked so comfortable on her, so warm and worn in, you'd have thought she'd been swaddled in it at birth. Over everything she sported what looked like a man's-size blue blazer from Brooks Brothers—Toby's perhaps—with the sleeves rolled up to her wrists, exposing the silky lining beneath. On her shoulder, she carried a red L. L. Bean book bag, and, in her free hand, a large green shopping bag from Benetton.

"I brought a prop!" she announced. "I hope that's all right."

I couldn't have spoken even if I'd wanted to, my teeth were chattering so badly from the cold. Instead, like some pervert, I nodded toward the park's entrance and led her to one of the benches inside. She had fretted for days about the monologue, she confessed, complaining that "a little more notice wouldn't have sucked" and had pored over all the plays she could get her hands on, Shakespeare and Strindberg and Shaw, arriving finally at her choice. "In the end," she said somberly, "I had to go with Wilde." It was a risky piece, but she'd practiced with friends all night over the phone and felt sure she had it down. She got up from the bench, reached into the Benetton bag—"I made this myself," she explained—and removed the thing inside.

It was one of those Styrofoam heads people display wigs on, and this one *had* a wig, a brown, stringy mop of hair that Elsa had fastened with bobby pins and was caked with what looked like ketchup. With black Magic Marker she'd drawn a pair of eyes rolled skyward, over which she'd placed a pair of Groucho Marx glasses, the moustache carefully scissored off, for added effect. Below the nose she'd stuck a pair of bright-red Mr. Potato Head lips. She grabbed the head by the hair, cleared her throat—"Here goes," she said—then contorted her face disturbingly, assumed a Wicked Witch voice, and began:

Ah! thou wouldst not suffer me to kiss thy mouth, Iokanaan. Well! I will kiss it now. I will bite it with my teeth as one bites a ripe fruit. Yes, I will kiss thy mouth, Iokanaan. I said it. Did I not say it? I said it. Ah! I will kiss it now. But wherefore dost thou not look at me, Iokanaan? Thine eyes that were so terrible, so full of rage and scorn, are shut now. Wherefore are they shut? Open thine eyes! Lift up thine eyelids, Iokanaan! Wherefore dost thou not look at me?

At various points during the monologue, Elsa would flick her little tongue like a snake and rake the air with her free hand. Also disconcerting was how she kept her big blue eyes fixed not on the head, but on me. She ended with that memorable line, "Thou didst bear thyself toward me as to a harlot, as to a woman that is wanton, to me, Salome, daughter of Herodias, Princess of Judaea!" I had no idea what to make of the whole thing. Truth be told, I didn't understand a word of it. Luckily, the second she finished, a bum walking by stopped to clap. "Encore, beautiful!" he shouted. "Encore!"

This bought me some time to gather myself, and once collected I managed the appropriate combination of expert's gravity with a healthy dose of praise. I advised her to cut down on the tongue stuff, perhaps, and to address herself more to the head than the audience. Elsa took this criticism seriously, chin in one hand, Iokanaan under her other arm. Before her second try, she turned to the bum, who'd decided to watch this rehearsal, and said, "Excuse me, sir, but could you maybe *fuck off*?" After the third run-through, I had no choice: bone-cold, I clapped as heartily as the bum, told her that she'd nailed it, and then hurried her the three blocks to Donovan's office on 57th Street.

Thankfully, Donovan wasn't interested in having Elsa perform something dramatic. One glance at her all-American good looks and he was pretty much sold. He handed her some commercial sides to read and gave her a couple of minutes to get comfortable with them. When she was ready, he called out, "Action," and she said, "Freshen Up! The gum that goes . . . *squirt!*" about as well as I could've hoped. Donovan told her he'd take her on, that she of course needed some head shots ASAP, that the sooner he could send her out on calls, the better.

"So," Elsa said, "I got the job?"

"No," said Donovan. "But you do have an agent."

Elsa clapped her elbows-together clap. "And you'll just call me and send me out on these things?"

"Correct."

"*Then* what do I do?"

"Jacob here can explain that stuff." Donovan gave her a contract to show her father, whose signature Elsa later forged. "It's old hat to him."

It was dark by the time we left Donovan's office, and, by now warmed up, I was happy to walk as slowly as possible to Elsa's bus stop. She was ebullient about the audition, although admittedly disappointed she didn't get to do her monologue. I had things I wanted to say to her. I just didn't know what they were.

"I really appreciate you taking time off from soccer practice to help me with this," Elsa said. "I really want to make some of my own money, so I don't have to depend anymore on my bastard father."

I told Elsa she didn't have to worry, that she'd probably make so much money doing commercials that she could pay her way through college.

"And I'd really be grateful," she went on, "if you kept coaching me on the whole process. Because I think it helped me up there."

Also no problem, I told her. Most of the time, I lied, we'd have auditions at the same places. All she had to do was phone me the night before she had a call, and I'd make sure to meet her beforehand. "You'd *do* that?" she asked. I would, I told her. We could go over lines and I'd show her the ropes. "That would be *so* excellent," she said. Elsa was by then accustomed to men doing anything for her, simply in order to be near her, but this was new territory and, like Kyle, I don't think she suspected anything, as she would say in SAT-speak, *untoward*.

At least not at first.

During those inaugural weeks of Elsa's acting career, she phoned me every night before her auditions. "If the commercial's for Bonjour jeans, but I only have Jordache, does that hurt my chances?" (Possibly, I told her. Perhaps we should go to Bloomingdales and try on a pair?) Or, "If the commercial's for Burger King and I only eat McDonald's, do I need to be familiar with the Whopper?" (I'm sure we could find a Burger King somewhere en route.) I'd meet her at the agencies beforehand, she'd sign in and grab the sides, then we'd go off to a corner and practice her lines, if she had any; or, if the commercial called for her to, say, dance, we'd step into a hallway, maybe, where she could show me a couple of her disco moves. (Elsa had perfected a particular white-girl step, right knee and elbow swirling in and out in unison, followed by her left, each half loop accompanied by a crisp finger snap.) This was all innocent and novel to her at first. She was enthusiastic—she really thought I was giving her the inside dope—and even got a couple of callbacks and print jobs, which bolstered my position as a helpmate. It got to the point where I could even call her directly on her private line at home, an act that took tremendous nerve on my part, but which she encouraged, especially if she was trying out for a movie. She would read me my lines, so I could write them down and we could rehearse them.

"Boogie," she read, "when we were dating, did you care for me?"

"Sure I did."

"Not because you could do things to me, but because you cared?"

"Of course, Beth. There were plenty of girls for that, you know, if a guy wanted a pop. But I gotta tell you, you were real good."

"I was?"

"Believe me."

I advised that we rehearse such scenes over and over again, hoping for a segue to myself, but never finding one. All I could discuss was technique, and I was as specific as Strasberg. In between our talks and our afternoons together, I was assailed by more fantasies of us becoming a couple, of the two of us walking hand in hand, this time in Central Park (sweaters again), or of me saving her from a mugger, my face ultimately replacing Toby's on her magnificent Wall of Self. Though what I remember most vividly during this time is my awareness of the gap between my success at getting us alone together and the romantic daydreams this engendered. It wasn't simply that I didn't know how to get from point A to point B with Elsa. No, it was a deep-seated recognition that even if I did, it wouldn't matter. I had knowledge of preordained defeat that it was in my character to ignore until the end.

Which came pretty soon. Within a month or so, I began to notice a diminishing enthusiasm for our telephone Q & As, until finally one night she explained that her audition tomorrow was for Finesse shampoo and, let's face it, she didn't need any help pretending to wash her hair. "Look, Jacob, nothing personal, but I'm acclimated to the process," she explained.

"What does that mean?"

"That I'm not a neophyte."

"What does that mean?"

"That you don't need to meet me at these things anymore."

This I understood.

But I quickly moved on. It was a stupid crush, after all. A seventh grader's heart isn't constant; and truth be told, I was relieved that Kyle hadn't found out about my subterfuge.

Except Elsa didn't let it go. When I did happen to run into her at auditions, I was met with *disingenuousness,* even *contumelies* and *disparagement* at the coincidence.

"Soooooo," she said when I went over and said hi to her one afternoon. "What brings *you* here?" She was sitting next to a good-looking actor, Toby's age, I guessed, the two of them going over their lines; she elbowed him in the side.

"Starburst," I said.

"Ree-ly," she smirked. "What did you have to do?"

"I had to pretend to eat a Starburst and react to the refreshing fruit flavor."

"Oh? What was your line?"

"Wow!" I said brightly, "Mouth-watering orange!"

"Um hum." She pursed her little lips.

"Strawberry too!"

"My little brother's friend," she told the guy, knocking her shoulder against his. "He's *quite* the thespian."

And then she did something cruel. She exposed me to Kyle, revealing my coaching lessons, our talks on the phone, the arrangements I'd made for us to meet regularly, even the calls to her private line—omitting, along with sympathy, that she'd asked for my help. She was on the lookout for armor against Kyle's frequent digs at her lapse on the SATs (Princeton had rejected her early), and this was the perfect deflection.

"Have you been talking with my sister?" he asked me over the phone. "Have you been meeting her after school?"

To try to explain would have meant admitting to the thing boys scorn most mercilessly in their peers: ambition.

I said nothing.

"Rose, you're such a kike piece of shit. Do me a favor and stay away from her. In fact, stay away from me too."

He hung up.

It was the "kike" thing that sent me to my father.

The day following my fight with Kyle, my dad and I were recording an episode of *The Eternal Light,* a joy because I got to miss school, but a chore because it was a grind. We taped at NBC on 44th and Sixth on a gigantic soundstage designed to accommodate a whole orchestra and then some, with microphones shaped like ears of corn hanging on long wires from high ceilings that were curved and made of rich-looking wood, as if we'd been enclosed in a shell fashioned of mahogany. The far corners of the space were piled with old sound-effects stations, wooden contraptions like miniature lemonade stands to which clown horns, bicycle bells, triangles, and door knockers were attached. There were door frames that creaked intentionally, a police siren you wound with a crank, and an enormous Chinese gong that I was told by the director to never, *ever* hit lest I blow the speakers in the control room to smithereens, and that I dream of bashing to this day. In the stage's center, near the two main microphones, was an enormous table, and the cast would gather here to do a read-through of the script together, the director giving us notes and making last-minute edits. After our lunch break we did two back-to-back hour-long recordings of the program straight through, no cuts. For all intents and purposes it was a live performance, so you had to follow the script carefully as the program proceeded in order not to miss your entrance (you'd get up from the table as quietly as possible, cautious not to rustle the pages of your script while tiptoeing to the mike), a lapse that could ruin a whole taping. The mikes were so sensitive they'd pick up a whisper; and because editing capabilities were limited, you couldn't make a mistake.

We were doing *The Chosen*, Chaim Potok's novel about an Orthodox boy, Reuven Malter, and his brilliant Hasidic friend Danny Saunders. I understood maybe a quarter of it, but I liked it even then, especially the baseball game at the beginning. I had a bit part as Davey Cantor, one of Reuven's teammates, and my lines were all a variation of "Wait till you see them, Reuven," referring to the opposing Hasidic team, "they're *murderers.*" But my dad was playing Reb Saunders, Danny's father, and perhaps because I badly needed his advice, I followed the story with interest. From what I could make out at the time, it was about two Jewish kids whose dads had different rules about being Jewish. I liked that after Danny hits a ball into Reuven's eye during the game, the two of them patch things up; it made me hopeful for Kyle and me. And I admired Danny's brilliance because it reminded me of Abe, in particular his ability to remember things in stories, and how when we read Shakespeare he could tell you page, act, scene, and line. Most of all, I enjoyed watching my father perform. At home he was often jumpy, distracted. It was hard to keep his attention. His mind wandered. He'd begin to talk and then trail off. If the phone rang ("That's probably the agency") he'd get up to take the call, even during dinner. But when he performed, he was a different person. He was focused. He listened to everything and didn't miss a cue. He possessed an authority that without lines was entirely absent. And when his time came to act he would quietly step to the mike with his script in his right hand, his left free to gesture, and he'd begin to speak as if through a prompter, with that distinct, more knowing voice-within-a-voice. Suddenly he was the deep, wise sound of reason; he *was* Reb Saunders. It was the oddest thing, but that was his gift: he read aloud and you believed him, even if he couldn't explain later what it was he'd uttered so eloquently.

But because there was so much of the play I *didn't* understand, so many basics, I needed his help. What was the Talmud? Gematria? Zionism? *Smicha?* It was like Abe's bar mitzvah, but without Abe. It was overwhelming, like reading through Swiss cheese. My father couldn't explain a lot of it, which was fine. I could accept all the unfamiliar terminology, but what I found most confusing was how Reb Saunders refused to talk to Danny.

"He's training him," my father explained. "He's training him to become a tzaddik." We were taking a cab home, something my father splurged on only after a full day of work. It was well past six and the traffic was bad. When my father said *tzaddik,* he stressed the first syllable, making a sound like *ts* and then pronouncing the *z*.

"What's that?"

"It's like a religious leader. That's what Reb Saunders is. He's a powerful rabbi."

"Oh," I said. "So he's a *Reb*."

"Exactly."

"What about *Nu*?"

"*Nu*. It's Yiddish. Let's see. *Nu* is like . . . it's like the word 'well.' You'd say, 'Well, when do we eat?' Some Jews say, '*Nu*, when do we eat?' "

"So why not talk to him?"

"Reb Saunders? To Danny?"

"Yes."

"Because he wants his son to suffer. He expects his son to take his place one day as tzaddik, and only someone who has suffered can feel the pain of the people he leads."

I thought about this for a while. "You made a good Reb," I told him.

My father turned to me, smiling appreciatively. "Thank you."

"I'm glad you and I talk."

"I am too."

"*Nu*," I said, "what about *kike*?"

My father did a double take. "That wasn't in the show."

I told him Kyle had called me one, but it wasn't a big deal. When they got into fights, he called Abe that too.

My father considered this silently, then asked the driver to take us once around the park.

"What does it mean?" I asked.

"It doesn't mean anything. It's just a nasty word for Jew."

"Have you ever been called one?"

"Yes. In the navy." The memory seemed to shake him. My father had been a naval photographer on a destroyer during Korea, though from what he'd told me it seemed his convoy spent all of its time in Greece. "A lot of the Southern guys said it. Though most of the time they called me Burger."

"Why?"

"Because of my name."

I waited.

"Rosenberg," he said. "Rosen*burger*."

"Check."

My mother was from the South. We spent every Christmas in Birmingham, Alabama, with her family. My grandfather was a colonel, and at night he and my father drank Wild Turkey, which my grandfather poured out first into a measuring cup ("He's a diabetic," my mother tried to explain). Last year, after a dinner filled with talk about the upcoming presidential election, my father and I had gone on an errand to the supermarket for my grandmother, and he said to me, "Just so you know, I hate it down here. I hate *all* of these people." Now I understood why.

"When they called you kike, what did you do?"

My father smiled. "I took their picture."

"Why?"

"It calmed them down. It made them nice. I'd say, 'Bubba, let me take your picture. I'll send a copy to your mom. Or your girl.' "

"What did they call you after that?"

"After that they called me Nate."

"Where does it come from?"

"Nate?"

"*Kike.*"

"That's an interesting question. I asked my father that once." My grandfather, Zada, a man I'd never met, was already long dead. Babu, my grandmother, lived alone in Los Angeles. She and Zada had moved there when my father was fifteen, leaving him behind in New York with his uncle so he could attend Music & Art high school. I knew next to nothing of her either—I'd met her once—except that she was from someplace in Russia or Poland that I couldn't find on a map and had fled to America because of pogroms, which for years I thought were a race of people. For my birthday, she unfailingly sent me a $25 check in a Hallmark card. "He told me that it comes from the Yiddish word *kikel.* That means 'circle.' Jews, when they came to America, they signed their immigration papers with a circle instead of an *X.*"

"Why?"

"Because *X* is the sign of Christ."

My father sounded like Reb Saunders explaining this. I was impressed by how much he knew.

"Anyway," he continued, "the men on Ellis Island who registered them began calling them *kikels,* which then became *kike,* I guess."

"What did your dad do?"

"He was a furrier. He made furs. For coats."

"Did he make money doing it?"

"No, he was always broke."

Our cab drove up the long hill at the northernmost end of the park.

"What is a Jew?" I asked him.

He waited for a long time. "What do you think it is?"

I thought for a while. I couldn't say why, exactly, but when I imagined a Jew, I always pictured Abe's father. There was a photo of him in Abe's bedroom that I loved. He was in his infantry uniform, leaning against a lightpole smoking a cigarette. He had the coolest black moustache. Though his family had fled Germany before the war, many of their relatives had been killed. He was sixteen when he arrived in America and immediately enlisted in the army, lying about his age, "so he could kill Nazis," according to Abe. He had a scar over his right eye from when a Nazi sergeant kicked him in the face one day on the street when he was ten years old. Mr. Herman later captured this same Nazi behind enemy lines, tied him up, and "beat the living shit out of him," also according to Abe. But many years later, Mr. Herman himself told me he'd put two bullets in the man's head: "two eyes for an eye." He had a ton of these stories, though in truth I thought of Mr. Herman as a Jew mostly because I couldn't go to Abe's house on Fridays or during Passover, when his family withdrew and their apartment became a kind of impregnable fortress. I did get invited that December for the lighting of their menorah, when again Abe sang in Hebrew (which I thought must be the same as Yiddish). He put on his yarmulke and chanted at the candelabra, and perhaps because we all stood so close around him he seemed oddly self-conscious, less sure of himself than during his bar mitzvah, and he occasionally fumbled the words, a rarity for Abe. "If we blow into the narrow end of the shofar," declares a writer I love, "we will be heard far. But if we choose to be Mankind rather than Jewish and blow into the wider part, we will not be heard at all." I read this in college and felt angry with my father for leaving my Jewishness to me; I remember thinking I was doomed to live a life without spiritual direction or shape—but I no longer accept that, at least not completely. It is to the memories of Abe's chanting, of Kyle's apartment, of Elsa's tiny mouth, of my father's voice ("He," referring to Elvis and the tenth anniversary collector's set, "was the King!")—it is to *these* that I am bound back.

"A Jew is someone who knows things," I said.

"Like?"

"Like what to sing." Then I thought of Mr. Herman enlisting. "Like what to do."

"You know," my father said, "I was a cantor when I was your age. A singer in synagogue."

"You know all those words?"

"Yes," he said.

"Why did you stop?"

"Why did I stop?" my father repeated. "I stopped because everywhere we went, my father was always making me sing."

My father didn't sing much anymore, though one of my earliest memories was of watching him perform on television. It was *The Young People's Concerts,* hosted by Leonard Bernstein, and the opera was Beethoven's *Fidelio.* He played Rocco, singing in German, and that he could speak another language amazed me. When I asked my mother why he didn't speak it at home, she said he couldn't. He'd just memorized the sounds.

"He wanted that to be my career," my father continued. "My life. We had terrible fights about it."

My father and I never fought. I loved him. He was kind. He had a beautiful voice. And we looked *exactly* alike. He looked, as I think back now, like a Sephardic William Shatner, and tonight I didn't fear our similarity or think of it as a curse. I wanted to be just like him.

"Why was that so bad?" I asked.

"To be a cantor?" He shook his head. He had the same bewildered look on his face as he did, years later, when late one night I found him staring blankly at the living room wall. Money, I didn't know then, was worse than tight—all the voice-overs, the career-making national accounts, the GEs, AT&Ts, and Friskies Buffets were going to the Donald Sutherlands, Demi Moores, and Lauren Bacalls of the world, to people, it was reasoned, you subconsciously recognized. *"Nu,"* he answered softly, "I don't know now."

We'd do one more loop around the park, though silently this time. We passed the Tavern on the Green, and through the brilliant glass windows I could see a group of waiters gathered around a table and singing—"Happy Birthday!" I guessed. My father had taken me there, too, when I turned thirteen.

Kyle and I made up, of course. Boys can't stay mad at each other about girls for too long. That's a job for men.

And one day, Elsa softened toward me.

It happened at BBDO, a big ad firm on the East Side. The

main office was shaped like an enormous circle, with a wide spiral staircase running down the center—a compass rose with multiple rooms around its circumference out of which simultaneous auditions were run. It was a bustling place in the afternoons, and it wasn't surprising to step off the elevator to see, say, a herd of leggy models so beautiful they seemed a separate species of person, tightly packed on the couches by the receptionist's desk; or twins of every shape, color, and size; or Dwarfs, Little Nerds with Big Glasses, Cute Old Ladies, mothers with Angelic Infants, or Black People. This time it was Teenage Couples.

Nor was I surprised to occasionally run into my father at these calls, and sure enough he'd had an audition himself that day. I could see the group of voice-over men, sides in hand, each one sitting a chair apart from the others, silently mouthing lines to himself. My dad was standing in front of the receptionist's desk, talking with one of the casting agents before leaving. These were usually women of a certain type. They wore low-cut, tight-fitting tops; eyeglasses, whether they needed them or not; jeans tucked into leather boots; shoulder-length hair down to what Abe called their mom's-aged asses. They looked old but seemed younger in their brazenness, in their willingness to ignore fundamental rules of engagement— for example that my father was married, or that I was *right there.* When I came across him with these tan, raven-haired, braceleted women, they stood close and touched his arm or chest when he made them laugh. They took him by the chin and kissed his mouth to say good-bye—and he let them! This made me hate them and him enough to scream, but I always remained silent at dinner that night with my unwitting mother and brother. It had happened, I thought, after our talk, because my father *wasn't* a Jew. And when I saw him on this particular day, I added a word to my definition of what a Jew was: *committed*.

"This must be your son," the woman said.

"It is."

"You look *exactly* alike," she told me.

Elsa appeared out of nowhere.

"Thank God you're here," she said. "Quick, I think I've got it figured out." She took me by the hand—hers was as dry as snake-skin—and hustled me over to the sign-in sheet. She counted off the names on the list, crossed out one person's, and rewrote it at the bottom. She had me write mine, then hers, right below it. "Now," she ordered when we sat down together, "don't you dare leave my side."

She was so flustered it was hard to get her to explain what was going on, so instead I asked what the audition was for.

"It's for Big Red chewing gum. Open your mouth." I did as told, and she squirted me with Binaca. "We have to kiss."

You see, Elsa whispered, there were some *ree-ly* gross guys here, and no way was she going to kiss some putrid stranger. "So when in doubt," she said, "stick to what you know."

"Meaning what?" I asked.

"Meaning *you*, douche bag. I *know* you."

We sat there for a moment. Grateful, she knocked her shoulder to mine. "Plus if you were older, you'd only be half bad."

I laughed. I was the youngest boy there by far, but Elsa clung to my arm as if we'd been in love since grade school. Our names were finally called, and we entered the room. The casting agent stood behind a video camera and a klieg light, and when we stepped onto the slightly raised platform that functioned as a stage, she told us that on "three" we were to say our names directly into the lens, then turn to each other. On "action," we would kiss until she said "cut."

"And it has to be a passionate kiss," she emphasized. "The kind that makes me taste the Big Red gum in your mouths."

Like I said before, I was thirteen years old and on the cusp of many things: regret, for instance; wrong turns; manhood; disappointments galore. But I did something in that room that day that I've come to recognize is so rare as to be precious: *I got in the moment.* After we announced our names, the woman told Elsa to let her hair down. Elsa turned to face me and shook out her ponytail, and I watched her unabashedly while she teased it into a mane. The casting agent was only a voice to us, invisible behind that floodlit wall, so it was like being alone anywhere I could imagine, which was nowhere else than where I was right now.

"How do I look?" Elsa asked.

"You look good," I answered, and stared at her little mouth and then into her eyes.

"I'm warning you," she said. "No tongue."

"No tongue," I repeated, though I had no idea what she meant.

"And not a word of this to Kyle."

"Not a word," I agreed.

"So far as I'm concerned," she said, "this never happened."

"Right, it never happened."

But then it *was* happening, my dream suddenly laid out on a platter like John the Baptist's head.

"Easy squeezie," she said, trying to calm herself.

"Easy," I answered. But already edging toward her, I was able to smell her now—my ear bent to the call for action.

Ladies and Gentlemen

The hotel room's curtains seemed to be burning too brightly at the edges, and Sara cursed when she saw the digital clock next to her bed. Her flight out of Nashville, bound for Los Angeles, left at 7:30; it was 6:49. She'd managed to catch several flights over the years in miraculous fashion, but this would really set the record.

Luck, however, was on her side. A taxi was waiting for her when she arrived in the lobby, traffic was light out to the airport, she stepped right up to the e-ticket kiosk, and the security line moved so efficiently that she even had time to stop at Starbucks, texting her husband while the barista made her café au lait. New Yorkers like her lived for this sort of synchronicity. When the subway arrived the moment you stepped onto the platform or all the lights down Park Avenue switched to green as your cab approached, it felt as if you were somehow being watched over. The Southwest attendant was about to close the door when Sara stepped onto the plane.

She wasn't surprised to find most of the seats taken. She hated to sit in back, where the turbulence was most acute, and on principle refused to share her seat with any overlapping parts of a fat person. She certainly wouldn't sit next to anyone with a baby; she had two sons of her own and had suffered through enough hellish trips with Tanner and Rob to make her sympathetic, but only from afar. Her supreme pet peeve, however, was a middle seat, and the attendant in back, already buckled in, was pointing to one that also happened to be in the last row. Mr. Window, hidden behind his newspaper, was clearly very tall, and Miss Aisle was Hispanic, in her early twenties, and already fast asleep.

As if sensing her preference, Mr. Window lowered his paper and offered Sara his seat the moment she appeared. He was getting off in St. Louis, he said, but "they're full all the way to Los Angeles." The man was Gumby-thin and broad-shouldered. He didn't stand so much as unfold, broadening and elongating like one of her son's Transformers. Their exchange, followed by his help jamming her bag into the overhead bin, momentarily woke Miss Aisle, who stared at them uncomprehendingly, until Mr. Window, in another pleasant surprise, said, *"Disculpe, señora. Le voy a dar mi silla."*

"De nada," she answered, and got up.

The plane backed out of the gate the moment Sara got settled and, in keeping with this morning's magical timing, made a beeline for the runway and took off without delay.

Her elation rose as the plane climbed. She was headed to LA to meet a man, Thom McKnight, whom she'd kissed in college nearly two decades ago and hadn't seen since, until yesterday, though she'd thought about him with an odd frequency over the years. She remembered very few things about him: two years older, a lacrosse player, a preposterously bad singer in a punk band. What she *did* recall with a nearly breathless vividness—it recurrently haunted her dreams—was an evening that ended with Thom helping her climb the outer walls of the campus's ancient observatory. In the moonlight he slid back a segment of the clamshell dome, dropped into the dark void, and called up to her, his disembodied voice urging her to trust him, to grab the edge and then hang down. She lowered herself into that blackness, dangling for several harrowing seconds until Thom's hands firmly gripped her knees, tracing the shape of her thighs and waist, and she released her grip, touching the floor as softly as a ballerina set down by her partner. Afterward they kissed for hours, and it was so singularly for its own sake and so blissfully erotic that she would've been content to keep doing it until daybreak. But Thom had other ideas, and they left for her room. The night might've ended differently if her roommate hadn't also gotten lucky, which she and Thom soon discovered. He lived in an apartment on the other side of the campus and was exhausted, he claimed, so she simply said good night, confident that another tryst was inevitable. But the next time they met he was both remote *and* with a girlfriend, and thus their immediate future ended and the long haunting began.

Sara, a freelance writer for several national magazines, was in Nashville for *Vanity Fair* to interview Reese Witherspoon, who was in the new Martin Scorsese movie, *Cell*, about a rogue federal marshal, played by George Clooney, who oversees a group of relocated, high-profile witnesses. The program is organized into cells so none of the handlers could compromise its security, but Clooney's character suffers from a God complex. His charges are desperate for news from family and friends, and he violates every protocol by exchanging this for money and, in Witherspoon's case, sex. Like all Scorsese's films, this was a redemption story, almost

Old Testament in its dimensions, since Clooney portrays a father at once protective and terrible. When his reckless behavior tips off the Mob to his cell's location, he must reject his sinful nature in order to protect his own newfound family.

Sara was sure the film would mark Witherspoon's return to A-list stature. It was also a great get. She'd interviewed her before, found her whip smart, charming, and, most important, forthcoming. They'd enjoyed a long, productive lunch yesterday, and afterward Sara visited the set, where she was shocked to run into Thom. It turned out he was the film's assistant director, and as he gave her a quick tour they giddily caught up. He was extremely busy—married too—but one thing led to another and he asked her to dinner, an invitation she enthusiastically accepted. They ate at Ruth's Chris Steak House, right next to her hotel, and their conversation was nearly as breathless as their kissing had been twenty years ago. Dale, her husband, called during dessert. So did Thom's wife. "Working late," each said. "I'll call in the morning. Love you." She felt like a swimmer at Set. "You haven't changed at all," she told Thom, who looked absurdly young. It's all in the genes, he claimed; his grandparents on both sides had lived past a hundred. As for her, "Well," he said, "you've become something entirely more dangerous." She excused herself to go to the bathroom and, alone for a moment, checked her teeth in the mirror (*that fucking spinach*) and took a long, hard look.

She would follow this man right now, anywhere, no questions asked, though her reasons—she promptly listed them—were more complicated and manifold than her desire.

She was thirty-nine, though she occasionally felt fifty. She'd chosen a profession that condemned her permanently to homework and consequently was never *not* working. She looked forward to traveling alone because on the road she could bathe in peace, without the sound effects of her family. Away from them, finally, she felt bereft. Meanwhile, private school ran thirty-six thousand dollars a year, times two. Yesterday she was breast-feeding Rob and now he was six. Tanner, her first great love since her husband, used to live for the sight of her, but these days cared mostly about his father and Rafael Nadal. She wanted another child, if only to have a baby to hold again, to which suggestion Dale replied: "I'd like to retire with dignity." This was reasonable, of course, yet she was heartbroken. She thought the planet was self-immolating. She missed her husband desperately, in spite of the fact he was *right there,* or possibly because of it. She occasionally glimpsed his naked body and realized she felt nothing. She'd catch him staring at hers in the mirror, suspecting that he felt the same thing. She couldn't remember what she did the day before, though each went something as follows: get the boys ready for school; clean up the study enough to concentrate; conduct multiple phone interviews; do notebook dumps and transcription; return or delete e-mails; eat her meals standing up; have *no* exercise whatsoever; attend editorial meetings uptown, midtown, or downtown; arrive home to prepare Dale's dinner and *not* spit at him while he pours himself a drink, turns on the television, and promises to do the dishes so she can "be with the kids" (i.e., help them with their homework); put the boys to bed; wash her face and brush her teeth; burn with rage that she hasn't had a single moment to herself in eons. Understand, as she now did in this bathroom, that she had a year, perhaps two, in which she might still consider herself young.

Take something for yourself, she thought, while you still can.

Thom, waiting at the restroom door, took her in his arms and kissed her. There *is* such a thing as a time machine. They pressed their foreheads together and made plans. He had dailies to review but could get to her room by eleven. Though he was leaving for LA around lunchtime the following day, the whole morning was free and clear. "Then I'll hang the DO NOT DISTURB sign on the door," she said.

Back at the hotel, she fired her husband a text, knowing he'd be asleep. *Early meeting. Flight pushed back. Will call in the afternoon.* She showered, put on makeup, brushed her teeth twice, and waited.

But Thom didn't show. Just past midnight, he texted her: *Hung up. Complete cluster fuck. Here's a long shot: Come to LA tomorrow?*

It occurred to Sara that the corollary to her memories of their long-ago night together was a promise that if in some implausible future a rendezvous like the one they were planning presented itself—with agreed-upon limits, a thing both enduring and self-canceling—then it would be an abiding and nurturing secret she could always tell herself. Sinning, she'd be redeemed, because she would've wholly given herself to an experience and closed a circle that had remained open. What she'd never seriously imagined was that she could enjoy the consummation of this fantasy with its progenitor.

Yes, she wrote, then immediately made the arrangements. And in the morning, she unwittingly left the DO NOT DISTURB sign dangling on the door.

. . .

About a half hour into the flight, Mr. Window gently touched her wrist and mumbled something she couldn't hear.

Sara removed her earbuds. "Sorry?"

"I couldn't help noticing." He pointed to her laptop's screen. "You interviewed Reese Witherspoon?"

"I did." Normally she'd be in blow-off mode, but he was clearly so self-conscious about his height, sitting there so still and hunched, with his elbows tucked into his sides and his hands folded in his lap, that she felt she owed him her attention. And he'd been such a gentleman earlier, giving up his seat.

"She's doing that movie in town," he said.

"*Cell.* I read the script. It's amazing."

"I'm glad to hear you think so."

"Why's that?"

"I wrote it."

He stated this matter-of-factly, with neither arrogance nor a hint of delusion, but Sara still couldn't help puckering her lips.

"What's your name?"

"Peter Handel."

She held out her palm. "License, pal."

He straightened a full two feet stuffing his hand down his pocket, then offered her his ID.

She promptly returned it. "Unbelievable."

"That's what I said when they picked the director."

"Didn't I read in *Variety* that it was a two-picture deal?"

"That's correct."

"The other's in production too, isn't it?"

"You're looking at a lottery winner."

"I'd have assumed a screenwriter with a couple green-lighted films wouldn't be flying coach, much less Southwest."

"After taxes and my agent's commission, I decided to give up the private jet."

"Still."

"Who knows? Maybe both movies'll tank and it's back to the day job."

"Which was?"

"Profesor de español."

"Duh," Sara said.

Peter's features were angular, his cheeks indrawn: he was very blond, almost towheaded, and his bangs hung boyishly over his light eyes.

Sara gave him her card, promising to send him the article. "You must be crazy doing rewrites," she added.

"I've flown more miles this year than in my entire life. But hey, who's complaining? The kids' college tuition is paid."

"Amen. How many?"

"Three. One by my first wife, two by my second."

"How is that?"

"The second marriage, or having three kids?"

"Both, I guess."

"The second marriage is good, thanks, though our two daughters are only fourteen months apart."

"How old?"

"Four and three."

"Yikes."

"When people saw Cynthia with a baby bump and an eight-month-old, they'd ask me when we found out we were pregnant again. To which I'd answer, 'When I came home and she started throwing shit at me.' "

Sara laughed. "I cannot imagine."

"It's like having one big baby, really. Except its right side is underdeveloped and sort of drag-foots along."

The attendant handed Sara her orange juice, then Peter his Coke.

"As for my first daughter, Maxine—"

"Great name."

"Thanks."

"By the first marriage?"

He nodded. "The divorce hasn't been easy on her. She's eleven now—we were very young when she was born—and she misses me. Also blames me for the entire thing. She lives with her mom in St. Louis. Glenda wanted to be near her family after we split, so I'm between here and there pretty often."

"That must be hard."

"It is. But I'm flush with Southwest drink coupons, and introducing Max to George Clooney and Zac Efron has healed many wounds."

"Efron's in the other film?"

"Can I tell you a secret? I had *no* idea who he was until last year."

"You *are* a lottery winner."

"Yet I remain humble and hardworking."

"Maybe I should be interviewing *you.*"

"I kind of thought you were."

"So tell me about the movie."

"It's called *Fifty States*. It's about a kid who in his freshman year of high school meets his true love, but they split up because his father's a traveling salesman and he ends up going to school in all fifty states. To deal with his heartbreak, he takes on the identity of each place he lives, so in DC he runs for class president, in Montana he becomes a cowboy, in Hawaii a surfer. Anyway, his true love's a military brat who travels all over too, and by a complete fluke they reunite in South Beach, where Efron's gotten into the club scene and decided to assume his most daunting identity yet."

"Which is?"

"Drag queen."

Sara chuckled. "Complications ensue."

"The last act's like *Some Like It Hot* and *The Birdcage* rolled together."

Smiling, she stared out the window at the green-brown quilt of farmland, not a single road in sight. She forgot for a moment where she was going and why. The thought of Rob, her second child, came to her, how he'd often appear at her desk, ask if she was still working, and then sit facing her after she'd lifted him onto her lap, slapping her cheeks with his palms. "All right," she'd tell him. "I can take a break." He'd lay on her chest, or she'd turn him around to watch the screen as she typed. She loved to smell his scalp, especially when it was hot and slightly sweaty, his scent revivifying her. She then considered Tanner, whom last week she'd watched play tennis with Dale, himself pretty accomplished, at the Central Park courts, chuckling when he aped Nadal's mannerisms before every serve, fastidiously tucking his hair behind his ears as he stood at the line. His strokes were still herky-jerky, but three years from now, she thought, he'd be trouncing Dale. She recalled one crosscourt blast so viciously angled it made his father drop his racquet and applaud, looking at her as if to share this harbinger of his doom, a gesture that also gave her a sense of her husband as a boy himself. The three of them walked back to the apartment together, and to her amazement Tanner held hands with them both, and Dale pressed a finger to his lips when she glanced up. She tried to pinpoint the last time they'd made love and was surprised she could. It was about two weeks ago, on a Saturday night, after the opening of the New York Film Festival. They often found each other like this, emerging from dreams, and there was something so purely efficient about their foreplay, the opposite of rote, that enclosed them and reminded her of why they'd fallen in love, the shape and stiffness of Dale's cock as familiar to her as her own hand, the length of their lovemaking perfectly adapted to their middle age, their endurance, and their ever-so-slightly-waning need for this pleasure, its variation over time as subtle and unnoticeable as the changing shape of a spouse's face.

"Is that why you're going to St. Louis?" Sara asked. "To see your daughter?"

"Actually," Peter said, "my ex-father-in-law's getting remarried."

"And you're attending the wedding?"

"Yup."

"You, sir, are one rare bird."

"Hey, I love the guy. I was as sad to lose him as I was my wife."

"It doesn't sound to me like you did."

"No, but it changed things."

"Is your father alive?"

"Yes, but we aren't close. We're very different."

"How so?"

"Too long a story to tell," he said.

Here, she thought, was a nerve best left alone.

"Anyway, my father-in-law and I just connected, you know? We played a lot of golf together too. He has three daughters himself and was thrilled to have another guy around. But he's had terrible luck with women until now."

The captain asked everyone to check their seat belts; they'd be landing in St. Louis shortly.

"Is this his second marriage?"

"His fourth. His first wife, my ex's mother, committed suicide. She was bipolar and shot herself—with his rifle, no less. He returned from a business trip to find her dead in their gazebo. She'd been up and down psychologically for years but lately seemed to have turned a corner, on a new medication, and then . . ." He snapped his fingers. "They found fifteen notes for friends and family in his study. She'd been planning her death for months."

"That's terrible."

"It gets worse. Less than a year later he got remarried, to a true saint who taught at my wife's elementary school, and she got killed in a car accident only months after the ceremony. Not surprisingly, he went into emotional lockdown afterward, which only made him a more desirable bachelor."

"Why's that?"

"Because women love a challenge."

"Are you really going to hit me with the myth of the unattain-
able man?"

"It's been my experience that only two kinds of men succeed
with women: those who hate them, and those who love them."

"Don't forget those who happen to be *rich*."

"Well, he's also really successful. He began in the trucking
business but then started a logistics company that coordinates
the transportation of temperature-sensitive materials all over the
world."

"Maybe you should introduce him to me."

"You're both already taken. Anyway, where was I? Ah. Tragedy
temporarily made him a hater, so—"

The plane touched down. The sky had gone gray and the flags
along the runway were puffed conical with the breeze.

"Oh, well," Peter said. "I'll save it for another flight. Suffice it
to say that after marrying a gold-digging harridan—and there's a
really Gothic story, mind you, with affairs and drug dealers and
people getting wired by the FBI—he finally met a woman whom
he loves and who loves him back."

"I'm glad."

"Me too. Wow."

"What?"

"That went fast. I talked a lot."

"I asked a lot of questions," Sara said.

"This always happens to me on flights. It's like therapy. The
honesty. The openness."

"It's the anonymity. It lowers your defenses. Plus I'm a professional."

"Clearly."

They'd arrived at the gate, the signal gonged, and passengers immediately filled the aisles. It always tickled Sara, this hurry to *stand*.

"One more question," she said.

"All right."

"Why did your first marriage end?"

Peter seemed to have anticipated this, rubbing his upper lip while considering his answer.

"Actually," Sara said, "I'm sorry. That was inappropriate."

"Don't apologize. The truth is, I wouldn't have time to tell you the whole story even if I was going on to LA."

She touched his forearm, and he glanced at her fingers resting there. He shook his head, shrugging, crossed his arms, and leaned toward her. "I had an affair," he said, lowering his voice. "Which is cart before the horse, okay? It wasn't the reason, I mean." He cleared his throat. "The reason, the *reasons*. The fucking *lack* of reason. Maybe it's a guy thing, but in spite of all the fights my ex and I had, all the problems and the history, I'll tell you what: the moment I slept with this other woman, I knew my marriage was over." There was bitter resignation in his voice. Then he stood up, towering above everyone around them. "Anyway," he said, "good luck."

Perhaps thirty passengers deplaned, and while the attendant took a head count and the cleaning crew made its pass, Sara turned on her BlackBerry. She had ten e-mails already and a text from Dale: *Where r u?*

Complications ensue, she thought, though the blowback from her husband's question was fiercer than she'd anticipated. Where *was* she headed? What if this meeting with Thom—this man, this stranger—became, instead of a permanent comfort, its opposite, an affliction, a widening fissure that sowed cynicism, supplying half-truths as answers to the most innocent questions before they were even asked? There would be many stories to tell, after all, starting *now*, followed immediately by a question: "Are you committed?" Was commitment the comfort, the balm? Because she could tell a good story, she was a demon with details, but first she had to *believe* in it.

Then, with uncanny synchronicity, a call came from Thom. *Unknown Number,* her screen said, with two choices given below: *Answer. Ignore.* She pressed the latter and remained seated. Group A was just boarding. She could get off here, in St. Louis, catch a flight to LaGuardia, and be home. She could forgive herself for Thom, for the kiss, for all of it. No harm, no foul. Yet it was the possible regrets that troubled her most, no matter what choice she made, the ones that would come to her later, in the night, and gnawed at her even now—starting with what you didn't take versus what you did. Not to mention the stories she might tell a future stranger about this moment, and what she'd decided before she was airborne again.

ACKNOWLEDGMENTS

Thanks, first, to Gary Fisketjon, for the best conversation there is. To Emily Milder, for her patience, humor, and incisive editorial comments. To Gabrielle Brooks, for keeping me on the radar. To Susanna Lea and Mark Kessler, for spreading the word. To Paul Russell and Benjamin Taylor for their enduring wisdom. My deep gratitude to several readers who generously offered their time and thoughts on these stories when they were in various stages of completion: Ben Abraham, Pamela Carver, Phoebe Carver, Dr. Dan Canale, Bill Ditenhafer, Bruce Dobie, George Erikson, Diana Fisketjon, Jon Glover, Rhonda Hart, Alex Hoblitzelle, Sally Mabry, Betsy Malone, Amanda McGowan, Kalen McNamara, Adam Michael, Nick Paumgarten, Alissa Reiner, Jim Ridley, David and Carden Simcox, Grace Tipps, Frank Tota, Kelly Williams, and Mike Witmore. To my parents, for countless reasons. Finally, to Beth, who made it all possible.

A NOTE ON THE TYPE

The text of this book was set in Ehrhardt, a typeface based on the specimens of "Dutch" types found at the Ehrhardt foundry in Leipzig. The original design of the face was the work of Nicholas Kis, a Hungarian punch cutter known to have worked in Amsterdam from 1680 to 1689. The modern version of Ehrhardt was cut by the Monotype Corporation of London in 1937.

Composed by North Market Street Graphics, Lancaster, Pennsylvania
Printed and bound by Berryville Graphics, Berryville, Virginia
Book design by Robert C. Olsson